王烨 梁媛 等 编

新概念英语 2

高频词汇 步步为赢

中国水利水电出版社
www.waterpub.com.cn

内 容 提 要

《新概念英语2高频词汇步步为赢》是针对《新概念英语》（新版教程）词汇同步学习而精心设计，囊括《新概念英语》单词表所有单词及课文中的重要词汇。从词语用法、精彩例句、语法知识、词组短语、词语辨析、谚语俚语、联想记忆等角度，帮助读者彻底记忆和掌握每一个单词。

本书能有效弥补教材生词表中仅给出词义的不足，强化学生对生词的理解，供读者检验和巩固所学知识。

本书适用于学习《新概念英语》（第二册）的读者。

图书在版编目（CIP）数据

新概念英语2高频词汇步步为赢 / 王烨等编. -- 北京 : 中国水利水电出版社, 2009.11
ISBN 978-7-5084-6994-2

Ⅰ. ①新… Ⅱ. ①王… Ⅲ. ①英语－词汇－自学参考资料 Ⅳ. ①H313

中国版本图书馆CIP数据核字(2009)第212043号

书　　名	新概念英语 2 高频词汇步步为赢
作　　者	王烨　梁媛　等　编
出版发行	中国水利水电出版社 （北京市海淀区玉渊潭南路 1 号 D 座　100038） 网址：www. waterpub. com. cn E－mail：sales@waterpub. com. cn 电话：(010) 68367658（营销中心）
经　　售	北京科水图书销售中心（零售） 电话：(010) 88383994、63202643 全国各地新华书店和相关出版物销售网点
排　　版	贵艺图文设计中心
印　　刷	北京市地矿印刷厂
规　　格	145mm×210mm　32 开本　7.875 印张　252 千字
版　　次	2009 年 11 月第 1 版　　2009 年 11 月第 1 次印刷
印　　数	0001—5000 册
定　　价	**18.80** 元

前 言 Preface

《新概念英语》在当今的英语图书市场影响很大，成为一套风靡全球的经典英语教程，同时受到了世界各地英语学习者的青睐，也在中国的英语学习者中赢得了无可比拟的盛誉。1997年推出的《新概念英语》（新版教程），更加注重对学生英语听、说、读、写四项基本技能的培养，更加符合中国英语学习者的特点和学习习惯。

很多人在学习新概念英语的同时，也期待能有一套同步辅导资料帮助他们更好地理解掌握新概念英语书中的内容。因此本套丛书也就应运而生了。

《新概念英语》注重听、说、读、写、译的全面提升，而词汇则是构建完美英语的基石。全面扎实掌握好词汇是学好英语的法宝，相信通过本书的学习，能够帮助不同年龄层、不同起点的学习者进入英语学习新境界。

《新概念英语2高频词汇步步为赢》是针对《新概念英语》（新版教程）词汇同步学习而精心设计，囊括《新概念英语》每册单词表所有单词及课文中的重要词汇。从词语用法、精彩例句、语法知识、词组短语、词语辨析、谚语俚语、联想记忆等角度，帮助读者记忆和掌握每一个单词。具体来说，本书有以下几方面的特色。

核心用法：详细介绍每个词汇的核心用法，包括核心词义、高频搭配、同类辨析等内容。

语境记忆：针对每个单词的最核心词义给出经典例句，帮助读者用语境记忆单词。

拓展用法：拓展单词的词性和词义，加深对单词的全面认识。

本丛书词汇各栏目内容丰富、实用，让考生在实践中领会、理解，从而记忆词汇。相信通过本套丛书的学习，能让读者更好地理解掌握新概念的教材内容，突破英语词汇难关，步步为赢！

　　本书由王烨、梁媛编写，马云秀、王建军、王海娜、王越、白云飞、刘梅、张世华、张红燕、张娟娟、张静、李光全、李良、李翔、李楚、陈仕奇、罗勇军、姜文琪、董敏、蒋卫华等同志在资料收集和整理方面做了大量的工作，在此一并向他们表示感谢。

编者

2009 年 9 月

目 录 Contents

Lesson

1

A private conversation
私人谈话

---

private [ˈpraivit]

核心词义	a. 私人的	The President is paying a private visit to Europe. 总统正在对欧洲作私人访问。
拓展词义	a. 秘密的, 私有的	Don't repeat what I've told you to anyone, it's private. 不要向别人转述我告诉你的事，这是保密的。

---

conversation [ˌkɔnvəˈseiʃən]

核心词义	n. 谈话	Conversation is one of pleasures of life. 交谈是人生一大乐趣。
习惯用法	in conversation with（在）和……谈话	

---

theatre = **theater** [ˈθiətə(r)]

核心词义	n. 剧场，戏院	Her mother never went to the theatre. 她母亲从不去戏院看戏。

---

seat [siːt]

核心词义	n. 座位	Do I have to reserve a seat? 我一定要预订座位吗？
拓展词义	v. 使就座	The usher seated us in the front row. 引座员让我们在前排就座。
习惯用法	be seated（口语）坐 take one's seat 就座，坐在自己的座位上	

play [plei]

核心词义	n. 游戏，比赛；戏	The college drama society is going to put on a play. 大学戏剧协会正准备上演一个剧目。
拓展词义	v. 玩（耍），游玩	They are playing with a ball. 他们在玩球。
习惯用法	play at 玩，打球，下棋，打牌 play with 玩，戏弄，摆弄	

loudly [laudli]

核心词义	ad. 高声地，大声地	Mary sings loudly and happily. 玛丽大声快乐地唱歌。

angry ['æŋgri]

核心词义	a. 生气的；愤怒的	My friends' angry words hurt my feelings. 我朋友的气话伤害了我的感情。
习惯用法	be angry with sb. 生某人的气 be angry about/at sth. 因某事而生气	

angrily ['æŋgrili]

核心词义	ad. 气愤地	He stumped angrily out of the room. 他气愤地跺着脚走出了房间。

attention [ə'tenʃən]

核心词义	n. 注意，留心；（口令）立正	Our attention was held throughout his long talk. 我们始终专心听着他的长篇大论。

bear [beə]

核心词义	v. (bore, borne) 容忍，忍受	She was unable to bear. 她忍受不了啦。
拓展词义	v. 承担，负担 n. 熊	His shoulders can bear a heavy load. 他的肩膀能挑重担。

习惯用法	bear away 夺取 bear down 击败，压倒 bear on 依靠；与……有关，对……有影响 bear up 打起精神，鼓起勇气 bear with 容忍；忍耐	

business ['biznis]

核心词义	*n*. 商业，生意；事	The insurance business is built on trust. 保险业建立在信任的基础上。 The company has done business with many countries. 该公司与许多国家做生意。
习惯用法	go to business 上班 in business 在做买卖 make business of 以……为业 out of business 失业，破产 have no business to do sth. 没有做（说）某事的权利	

rudely ['ru:dli]

核心词义	*ad*. 无礼地，粗鲁地	He broke rudely into our talk. 他粗鲁地打断了我们的谈话。

Lesson

2

Breakfast or lunch?
早餐还是午餐？

until [ən'til]		
核心词义	*prep*. 到…… 为止，在…… 以前	She couldn't speak until she was two. 直到两岁她才会说话。

outside ['aut'said]		
核心词义	*ad*. 在外面	It's quite dark outside, there's no moon. 外面很黑，没有月亮。
拓展词义	*prep*. 在……外 *a*. 外部的 *n*. 外部	All the outside doors have locks. 所有外面的门都上了锁。 The door was locked on the outside. 那扇门从外面锁上了。
习惯用法	outside of 在……外面，超出……范围	

ring [riŋ]		
核心词义	*v*.（rang, rung） 发出响声	Just as I was opening the front door, the telephone rang. 正当我开前门的时候，电话响了。
拓展词义	*n*. 环形物，环状，铃声	She wears a pair of pretty ear rings. 她戴着一副漂亮的耳环。 I will give you a ring tonight. 今天晚上我给你打电话。
习惯用法	a wedding ring 结婚戒指 give sb. a ring 给……打电话	

aunt [ɑ:nt]

核心词义	n. 伯母，姑，婶，姨，舅母，大娘，大妈	She is a good aunt to all the children in the neighborhood. 她是街坊上所有孩子的好阿姨。

repeat [ri'pi:t]

核心词义	v. 重复，复述	Will you repeat that question, please? 请重复一下那个问题好吗?
拓展词义	n. 重复，反复	I'm tired of seeing all these repeats on television. 那些重复的电视节目我都看腻了。

Lesson

3

Please send me a card
请给我寄一张明信片

---

send [send]		
核心词义	*v*.（sent, sending）送，寄，发送	She sent for the doctor. 她派人去请医生。
习惯用法	send back 送回，发回，退回 send for 派人去请，召唤，索取 send in 呈报，提交，送来 send somebody off 为某人送行	

postcard [ˈpəustkɑːd]		
核心词义	*n*. 明信片	I bought a postcard yesterday. 昨天我买了一张明信片。

spoil [spɔil]		
核心词义	*v*.（spoiled or spoilt）使索然无味，损坏	The heavy rain has spoilt the flowers in the park. 这阵大雨把公园里的花全浇坏了。
拓展词义	*v*. 溺爱，宠坏	His grandmother spoiled him. 他的祖母把他宠坏了。

museum [mju(ː)ˈziəm]		
核心词义	*n*. 博物馆	You won't see live animals in a museum. 在博物馆里你不会看见活的动物。

public [ˈpʌblik]		
核心词义	*a*. 公共的，公众的	It is a matter of great public interest. 这是一个公众普遍关心的问题。

拓展词义	*n*. 公众，大众，民众	The public is/are the best judge. 公众是最好的裁判。

friendly [ˈfrendli]

核心词义	*a*. 友好的	She is friendly to my boyfriend. 她对我的男朋友很友好。
习惯用法	be friendly to... 对……很友好；赞成……的	

waiter [ˈweitə]

核心词义	*n*. 招待员，服务员	The waiter didn't understand English. 那个服务员不懂英语。

lend [lend]

核心词义	*v*. (lent，lent) 借给，贷款	He neither lends nor borrows. 他既不借给人也不向人借。
词语辨析	borrow 和 lend 都含借的意思。 borrow 指（从主语的角度讲）借进，表示从（向）……借……，自己暂时使用；lend 指把……借给，表示将自己的东西暂时借出给别人。	

decision [diˈsiʒən]

核心词义	*n*. 决定，决心	Several unpopular decisions diminished the governor's popularity. 几项不得人心的决定使州长的声望下降。
习惯用法	make a decision 下定决心，做出决定	

whole [həul]

核心词义	*a*. 整个的	The whole village was attacked with influenza. 整个村子的人都得了流行性感冒。
拓展词义	*n*. 全部	The whole of my money was stolen. 我全部的钱都被偷走了。

single [ˈsiŋgl]

核心词义	*a*. 单身的，唯一的，单一的，个别的	The letter was written on a single sheet of paper. 这封信只用一张纸写成。

Lesson

4

An exciting trip
激动人心的旅行

exciting [ik'saitiŋ]		
核心词义	a. 令人兴奋的	He concentrated his pupils and declared the exciting news. 他把他的学生集中在一起，宣布了这条令人兴奋的消息。

receive [ri'si:v]		
核心词义	v. 收到，接受	Our TV receives well since we had a new antenna put on. 自从安装了新天线以来，我们的电视接收良好。
拓展词义	v. 忍受，受到	The report received accolades from the press. 这篇报道受到新闻界的赞扬。
词语辨析	receive, accept 都含收到、接受的意思。receive 指收到，着重行为本身，而不涉及收受者是否接受；accept 指领受、接收，着重除行为本身以外，还表示接受者经过考虑以后愿意接受。	
联想词汇	perceive [pə'si:v] v. 察觉，感觉，理解 deceive [di'si:v] v. 欺骗，行骗	

firm [fə:m]		
核心词义	n. 商行，公司	The firm has agreed to give me a two weeks' holiday. 公司已经同意给我两个星期的假。
拓展词义	a. 坚定的，坚固的 v. (使) 变得坚实	The runner has firm muscles. 那个赛跑运动员有一身结实的肌肉。

different [ˈdifrənt]

核心词义	a. 不同的	He's a different man from what he was 10 years ago. 他和 10 年前不一样。
习惯用法	be different from 与……不同	

center = centre [ˈsentə]

核心词义	n. 中心，中央	Beijing is the political，economic and cultural centre of China. 北京是中国的政治、经济和文化中心。
拓展词义	v. 集中，使集中在一点	Our thoughts centre on how to fulfill the sales plan this year. 我们的思绪都集中在如何完成今年的销售计划上。

abroad [əˈbrɔːd]

核心词义	ad. 在国外，到海外	We may go abroad for holidays. 我们可能到国外去度假。
习惯用法	at home and abroad 在国内外 be all abroad 茫然不解，感到莫名其妙 from abroad 从国外，从海外	

Lesson

5

No wrong number
无错号之虞

---

pigeon [ˈpidʒin]		
核心词义	n. 鸽子（家鸽）	Keeping carrier pigeons is his hobby. 养信鸽是他的业余爱好。

message [ˈmesidʒ]		
核心词义	n. 消息，信息，口信	Let's leave her a message to meet us at the railway station. 让我们留个口信，通知她到火车站去跟我们见面。
习惯用法	send sb. on a message 派……出去报信 leave a message 留个话	

cover [ˈkʌvə]		
核心词义	v. 越过	I want to cover 100 miles by dark. 我想在天黑之前走完 100 英里。
拓展词义	v. 覆盖，涉及，包含 n. 封面，盖子，表面	The town covers 5 square miles. 小镇占地 5 平方英里。 The review covered everything we learned last term. 这次复习包括上学期我们所学的全部课程。
习惯用法	be covered with 盖满，覆满，充满 under the cover of 在……掩护下	

distance [ˈdistəns]		
核心词义	n. 距离	Oil painting is to be appreciated at a distance. 油画要在一定的距离外欣赏。

拓展词义	*n*. 远处；时间相距	You can see the mountain in the distance. 你可以看见远处的山。
词语辨析	far，distant 都含远的意思。 far 通常只指空间上的远距离，只有在"How far?"这句问话中，才可指远距离或近距离，也用以指时间上的距离； distant 指远隔的，可表示时间、空间的远距离，指时间时距离可大可小，但当指极大的距离（如太阳与地球的距离）时，则用 distant，不用 far。	

request [riˈkwest]		
核心词义	*v*. 请求，要求	Workers requested a raise in the wage. 工人们要求提高工资。
拓展词义	*n*. 要求，请求	She made a request for giving her some money. 她请求给她点儿钱。
习惯用法	request sth. from sb. 向某人要求某物 make (a) request for 请求，要求	
词根词缀	词根 re-表示"再"的含义	

spare part [ˌspeəˈpɑːt]		
核心词义	*n*. 机器备件	I've been trying to raise this spare part everywhere. 我一直在到处寻找，想弄到这种备件。

service [ˈsəːvis]		
核心词义	*n*. 业务，服务	We flatter ourselves that we provide the best service in town. 我们相信我们提供的服务在本市最好。

Lesson

6

Percy Buttons
珀西·巴顿斯

beggar [ˈbegə]		
核心词义	n. 乞丐	He is no better than a beggar. 他实际上等于一个乞丐。
联想词汇	beg [beg] v. 请求，乞求	

food [fuːd]		
核心词义	n. 食物，粮食，食品	The food was both bad and insufficient. 食物既糟糕又匮乏。

pocket [ˈpɔkit]		
核心词义	n. 衣袋，小袋	My keys are in my coat pocket. 我的钥匙在外衣口袋里。
习惯用法	a deep pocket 富裕，殷实 out of pocket 赔钱；白花了钱的	

call [kɔːl]		
核心词义	v. 号召，打电话，拜访	The sirens are calling the men to assemble. 警报声在召令士兵集合。
拓展词义	v. 叫，请 n. 呼叫，访问，打电话	Are you calling me a liar? 你是在说我是个撒谎的人吗？ I heard a call for help. 我听到了呼救声。 He called me last night. 他昨晚给我打电话了。

习惯用法	call out 大声喊叫，召集 call on 拜访，要求，请求 call in 收集，收回 call back 召回，取消

Lesson 7

Too late
为时太晚

---

detective [di'tektiv]

核心词义	n. 侦探	The company hired a detective to investigate the accident. 公司雇佣了一名侦探来调查这次事故。
联想词汇	detect [di'tekt] v. 发现，发觉，查明	

---

airport ['εəpɔ:t]

核心词义	n. 机场	You must arrive at the airport two hours early. 你必须提前两小时到达机场。

---

expect [iks'pekt]

核心词义	v. 预期，盼望，期待	The journey was not as nice as we had expected. 这次旅途不像我们预想的那样好。
习惯用法	expect sth. of sb. 对……的期望	

---

valuable ['væljuəbl]

核心词义	a. 贵重的，有价值的	This is one of the most valuable lessons I learned. 这是我所学到的最宝贵的教训。

---

parcel ['pɑ:sl]

核心词义	n. 包裹	I am going to take the parcel to the post office this afternoon. 今天下午我打算去邮局寄包裹。
拓展词义	v. 把……打成包裹	The sales clerk parceled his purchase. 售货员把他买的东西包了起来。

diamond [ˈdaiəmənd]		
核心词义	*n*. 钻石	She wears a diamond ring on her left hand. 她左手上戴着一枚钻石戒指。

steal [stiːl]		
核心词义	*v*. (stole，stolen) 偷	He stole out of the house without anyone seeing him. 他悄悄地溜出了房子，却没有人看见他。
习惯用法	steal out (of) (从……) 偷偷溜出 steal off 偷去，拿跑 steal away (把某物) 偷走；溜掉；(时间) 不知不觉地过去	

main [mein]		
核心词义	*a*. 主要的	This is the main purpose of my coming here. 这就是我到这儿来的主要目的。
词根词缀	词根-tain 表示"保持"的含义	

airfield [ˈeəfiːld]		
核心词义	*n*. 飞机场	We must prolong the runway of the airfield. 我们必须加长机场跑道。

guard [ɡɑːd]		
核心词义	*n*. 守卫者，警戒	He wears the guard on his expression. 他脸部带有戒备的神情。
拓展词义	*v*. 保卫，看守	Three men guarded him whenever he went out. 每当他外出时都有三个人保护他。
联想词汇	guarantee [ˌɡærənˈtiː] *v*./*n*. 保证，担保	

precious [ˈpreʃəs]		
核心词义	*a*. 宝贵的，珍贵的	He has sent me most precious gifts. 他送给我极其珍贵的礼物。

stone [stəun]

核心词义	n. 石头，石块	Can you move the stone? 你能移走这块石头吗？
拓展词义	n. 矿石，宝石	Marble is a precious stone. 大理石是一种珍贵的石料。

sand [sænd]

核心词义	n. 沙子，沙滩	Sands are a large area of sand. 沙漠就是大面积的沙地。

Lesson

8

The best and the worst
最好的和最差的

---

competition [kɔmpi'tiʃən]

核心词义	n. 比赛，竞争	There will be a chess competition next week. 下个星期有一场国际象棋比赛。

neat [niːt]

核心词义	a. 整洁的，整齐的	Cats are neat animals. 猫是爱整洁的动物。
联想词汇	net [net] a. 净的，纯的 n. 网，网状系统	

path [pɑːθ]

核心词义	n. 小路，小径	Keep to the path or you may lose your way. 沿着这条路走，否则你会迷路的。
拓展词义	n. 路线，路径	The path of an arrow is a curve. 箭的轨迹是一条弧线。
词汇辨析	path，road，way 都含有"道路"的意思。 path 常常指只供人们步行的小路。 road 通常指人和交通工具通行的一条条的路。 way 指要达到特定的地点所必须通过的地方。	

wooden ['wudn]

核心词义	a. 木头的	The room was full of wooden furniture. 房间里摆满了木制家具。

pool [puːl]

核心词义	n. 水坑，水塘，水池	There were pools of water in the holes in the road. 马路上有许多水坑。

Lesson

9

A cold welcome
冷遇

welcome ['welkəm]		
核心词义	n./v. 欢迎	He welcomed you to enjoy his hospitality. 他欢迎你去做客。
拓展词义	a. 受欢迎的，可喜的	You are always welcome in my home. 你在我家总是受欢迎的。
习惯用法	You are welcome.（对方表示感谢时，常用的答语）不用客气，不用谢。	

crowd [kraud]		
核心词义	v. 拥挤，集聚	Swimmers crowded the beaches. 海滩上挤满了游泳的人。
拓展词义	n. 人群，一群人，观众	A crowd of people were waiting in the hall. 一大群人在大厅里等着。
习惯用法	a crowd of 一群，一堆 be crowded with 满是…… in crowds 成群，大群地	

gather ['gæðə]		
核心词义	v. 聚集，集合	The crowd is gathering. 人群正在聚集。
拓展词义	v. 收集，采集	We need to gather more information to research this case. 我们对这个案子需要收集更多的信息。
习惯用法	gather out 选出 gather together 集合，集聚，收集	

hand [hænd]

核心词义	n.（表或机器的）指针，手，协助	The hour hand is smaller than the minute hand. 时针比分针短。
拓展词义	v. 递，交付，传给	A doctor and a nurse are handing my father from the ambulance. 一个医生和护士把我父亲从救护车上扶下来。
习惯用法	on one hand... on the other（hand）一方面……，另一方面 hand in 交；提交 hand in hand 手拉手地；联合地 hand out 交出；分发	

shout [ʃaut]

核心词义	v. 呼喊，喊叫	The old lady shouted at the boy. 那个老太太冲着那个小男孩大声地喊。
联想词汇	shout out 大声嚷嚷	

refuse [riˈfjuːz]

核心词义	v. 不愿，拒绝	I can't refuse his request. 我无法拒绝他的要求。
习惯用法	refuse to do sth. 拒绝做某事	
词根词缀	词根-fuse 表示"注、流、倒"的含义	

laugh [lɑːf]

核心词义	v. 笑，发笑	We all laughed at his joke. 听了他的笑话我们都大笑起来。
拓展词义	n. 笑；笑声	He gave a good loud laugh when he saw it. 他一见到它便大笑。
习惯用法	have the last laugh 笑在最后，取得最后胜利 laugh at 因……而笑，嘲笑 laugh off 对……付之一笑，以笑来排除……	

	smile，laugh 都含有笑的意思。
词语辨析	smile 指无声的笑，通常表示愉快、亲切、友好等，有时也表示讥讽、嘲笑等。 laugh 指出声地笑，而且带有面部表情和动作，它可以表示高兴、快乐、嘲笑等。

Lesson

10

Not for jazz
不适于演奏爵士乐

---

jazz [dʒæz]

核心词义	*n*. 爵士乐	It was my younger brother who introduced me to jazz. 是我弟弟使我了解了爵士乐。

musical [ˈmjuːzikəl]

核心词义	*a*. 音乐的	He showed exceptional musical ability. 他显示出特殊的音乐才能。

instrument [ˈinstrumənt]

核心词义	*n*. 乐器，工具，仪器	Do you play an instrument? 你演奏乐器吗？ He is handy with any instruments. 他对任何工具的使用都很在行。
联想词汇	instruct [inˈstrʌkt] *v*. 教，命令，指导，传授	

clavichord [ˈklævikɔːd]

核心词义	*n*. 古钢琴，翼琴（钢琴的前身）	Our clavichord is kept in the living room. 我们的这架古钢琴存放在起居室里。

recently [ˈriːsəntli]

核心词义	*ad*. 最近	He has recently learned English. 他最近学习英语。

damage ['dæmidʒ]

核心词义	v. 损害，毁坏	The earthquake damaged several buildings. 地震使一些建筑受到了破坏。
拓展词义	n.（pl.）赔偿金，损坏	The court awarded £500 in damages to the injured. 法庭判给受伤者500英镑的赔偿费。

key [kiː]

核心词义	n. 钥匙；键，（乐曲的）调；题解	This piece changes key many times. 这首曲子有多处变调。 I don't know the key to the puzzle. 我不知道这个谜语的答案。 I've left my keys at home and can't get my books. 我把钥匙丢在家里了，我的书拿不着了。

string [striŋ]

核心词义	n. 线；（乐器的）弦	His fingers swept the strings of the guitar. 他的手指轻轻拂着吉他的弦。
拓展词义	n. 一串，一系列 v. 上弦	The youngsters set off string after string of firecrackers to mark Spring Festival. 孩子们放了一串又一串的鞭炮，以欢庆春节。 She can string a violin. 她会给小提琴上弦。
习惯用法	string on 把……串在……上 string up 悬挂，绞死	

shock [ʃɔk]

核心词义	v. 震惊，冲突，使……不高兴或生气	I was shocked when I heard about your accident. 我听到你的消息后感到很震惊。
习惯用法	expect sth. of sb. 对……的期望	

allow [əˈlau]

核心词义	v. 允许，准许，给予	This diet allows you one glass of wine a day. 这种规定饮食可让你每天喝一杯酒。
习惯用法	allow that... 承认…… allow of 容许；许可 allow for 考虑，顾及 be allowed to do sth. 允许做某事	

touch [tʌtʃ]

核心词义	v. 接触，触摸	That woman's sad story touched our hearts. 那位妇女的悲惨经历触动了我们的心弦。
拓展词义	n. 手感；手法；触摸 v. 感动	This material was soft to the touch. 这种料子手感很柔软。
习惯用法	in touch of 在……能达到的地方，在……的附近 out of touch with 同……失去联系，与……没有通信 touch on 与……有关系 touch with 用……触摸	

Lesson

11

One good turn deserve another
礼尚往来

---

turn [təːn]

核心词义	*n.* 行为，举止； *v.* 使旋转，转动	All he done is a good turn. 所有他做的是一个很好的行为。 The wheels were turning swiftly. 轮子飞快地转动着。
拓展词义	*n.* 方向改变；顺次 *v.* 改变方向；变为	He used to be a linguist till he turns writer. 他过去是个语言学家，后来成了作家。 My turn will come. 我的时运快来了。
习惯用法	in turn/ take turns 轮流的，依次 turn away 转过脸去，把……打发走 turn down 减小，拒绝 turn in 上交，呈交，归还 turn into 进入，使变成 turn over 使……翻过来，仔细考虑 turn to 转向，求助于 turn up 开大，出现 turn on 拧开（自来水、电灯、收音机等） turn off 关（自来水、电灯、收音机等）	

deserve [diˈzəːv]

核心词义	*vi.* 应该得到　He does not deserve your help. 他不值得你帮助。
习惯用法	deserve to 值得；应受；应该得到

lawyer [ˈlɔːjə]

核心词义	n. 律师	He was trained to be a lawyer. 他被培养成一名律师。

bank [bæŋk]

核心词义	n. 银行 v. 把……存入银行	He put away his savings in the bank at the end of every month. 他每月底去银行存款。
拓展词义	n. 堤，岸	The town stands on the left bank of the river. 城镇位于河的左岸。
习惯用法	bank up 堆起，堆积	

salary [ˈsæləri]

核心词义	n. 薪水	The salary they pay me is none too high. 他们付给我的薪水不太高。

immediately [iˈmiːdjətli]

核心词义	ad. 立即，马上，直接地	He lay down and was asleep immediately. 他躺下，很快地睡着了。

Lesson

12

Goodbye and good luck
再见，一路顺风

---

luck [lʌk]

核心词义	n. 运气，幸运	It was good luck that I met you here; I did not expect to see you. 我在这儿见到你真走运，我没想到会见到你。

---

captain ['kæptin]

核心词义	n. 船长	The sailors are asked to take their positions by their captain. 船长要求水手们各就各位。
联想词汇	capital ['kæpitəl] a. 资本的，主要的，大写的 n. 首都，资本，大写字母	

---

sail [seil]

核心词义	v. 航行；开船	When does the ship sail? 这艘船何时起航？
拓展词义	n. 帆，航行游览；航程	This port is within two days' sail of New York. 这个港口离纽约的航程不到两天。
习惯用法	set sail 开船，启航	

---

harbor ['hɑːbə(r)]

核心词义	n. 海港	The hotel overlooks the harbor. 那间旅馆俯瞰着港口。

proud [praud]

核心词义	a. 骄傲的，自豪的	My father is very proud of his new car. 我的父亲非常满意自己的新车。
习惯用法	be proud of 以……为骄傲，以……为自豪	

important [im'pɔːtənt]

核心词义	a. 重要的，重大的	He has just been called away to an important meeting. 他刚才给叫走去开一个重要会议。

Lesson

13

The Greenwood Boys
绿林少年

group [gruːp]		
核心词义	n. 团体，组	A group of students was waiting by the school. 一群学生在学校旁边等着。
习惯用法	a group of 一群，一组，一批 group around 围在……的周围	

pop singer [pɔp-'siŋə]		
核心词义	n. 流行歌手	Not long after that，she made a national name as a pop singer. 此后不久，她便成为一名全国闻名的流行歌手。

club [klʌb]		
核心词义	n. 俱乐部	He is an active member of the school's stamp club. 他是学校集邮俱乐部的一名活跃会员。

performance [pə'fɔːməns]		
核心词义	n. 表演，演出	The performances are on the 5th and 6th of this month.（剧的）上演是在这个月的 5 号和 6 号。

occasion [ə'keiʒən]		
核心词义	n. 场合	I only wear a tie on special occasions. 我只有在特殊的场合才系领带。

拓展词义	*n*. 机会； 理由	I want to take this occasion to thank you. 我想借此机会向你表示感谢。 There was no occasion to do so. 没有理由这样做。
习惯用法	on occasion 有时，不时，必要时 by occasion of 由于；因为	

Do you speak English?
你会讲英语吗？

amusing [ə'mjuːziŋ]		
核心词义	*a.* 有趣的，引人发笑的	Her behavior was very amusing. 她的行为非常好笑。

experience [iks'piəriəns]		
核心词义	*n.* 经历，经验	None of the others have lived my experiences. 没有任何人体验过我的经历。
拓展词义	*v.* 经历，体验，感受	She experienced a joy in helping others in trouble. 她感受到了帮助有困难的人带来的快乐。

wave [weiv]		
核心词义	*vi.* （挥手）示意，致意	He saluted his friends with a wave of the hand. 他挥手向他的朋友致意。
拓展词义	*v.* 飘扬，摇摆 *n.* 波涛，波浪，挥手	The grass waved in the wind. 草在风中起伏波动。 The waves are high. 波涛汹涌。

lift [lift]		
核心词义	*n.* 搭便车；举起；电梯	We got a lift part of the way in a lorry. 我们有一段路搭乘了卡车。 With one great lift, the men moved the rock. 那些人猛一抬把那块石头搬动了。

拓展词义	v. 拿起，搬起，举起	He can't lift the table. 他抬不起来这张桌子。

reply [riˈplai]

核心词义	v./n. 回答，答复	He gave me no chance to reply to his question. 他没有给我回答他问题的机会。
习惯用法	reply to 回答，答复 in reply（to）为答复……；作为对……的答复	
词根词缀	词根-ply 表示"折叠"的含义。例如 apply [əˈplai] v. 应用，申请	

language [ˈlæŋgwidʒ]

核心词义	n. 语言	The language this computer uses is BASIC. 这台计算机使用的是 BASIC 语言。

journey [ˈdʒəːni]

核心词义	n. 长途旅行，旅程，路程（常指陆路）；行程	I don't envy your journey in this bad weather. 我并不羡慕你在这样恶劣的天气里旅行。
词语辨析	journey，trip 都含旅行的意思。 journey 应用范围很广，指有预定地点的陆上、水上或空中的单程长、短途旅行，一般来说，它着重指长距离的陆上的旅行； trip 为一般用语，指任何方式的，从事业务或游览的旅行，往往着重于短途旅行，在口语中，可与 journey 互换。	

Good news
佳音

secretary [ˈsekrətri]		
核心词义	n. 秘书	It takes a new secretary one month to break in. 新来的秘书要一个月的时间熟悉工作。
拓展词义	n. 部长，大臣，书记	The President confirmed him as the Secretary of State. 总统任命他为国务卿。
习惯用法	the Secretary of State [美] 国务卿；[英] 国务大臣	

nervous [ˈnəːvəs]		
核心词义	a. 神经紧张的	She felt very nervous with so many people looking at her. 这么多人看着她，她感到非常紧张。
习惯用法	feel nervous about 不寒而栗，担心	

afford [əˈfɔːd]		
核心词义	v. 担负得起，花费得起	He can't afford to buy a car. 他买不起汽车。
习惯用法	can't afford to... 买不起……	

weak [wiːk]		
核心词义	a. 无力气的，虚弱的	Don't stand on that chair, it's got a weak leg. 那张椅子有一条腿不牢，不要站在上面。

| 拓展词义 | *a.* 软弱的，无说服力的 | That was an incredibly weak answer. 那是一个令人难以置信的缺乏说服力的回答。 |

interrupt [ˌintəˈrʌpt]

| 核心词义 | *v.* 打断 | Don't interrupt father when he's occupied with his newspaper. 父亲看报的时候不要去打岔。 |
| 词根词缀 | 词根-rupt 表示"突然发生、爆发，中断"。例如：abrupt [əˈbrʌpt] *a.* 突然的，唐突的 | |

Lesson 16

A polite request
彬彬有礼的要求

park [pɑːk]		
核心词义	v. (停放) 汽车	A car parked in front of the building. 楼房前面停着一辆车。
拓展词义	n. 公园	They were playing in the park. 他们正在公园里玩耍。

traffic ['træfik]		
核心词义	n. 交通	The newcomer is not used to the heavy traffic in big cities. 新来者对大都市拥挤的交通不习惯。
习惯用法	a traffic jam 交通阻塞	

ticket ['tikit]		
核心词义	n. 票，券；交通违规罚款单	The driver got a ticket for speeding. 司机超速行驶，接到违章罚单。 Please show your ticket to the stewardess when you board the plane. 登机时请向空中小姐出示机票。

note [nəut]		
核心词义	n. 笔记，便条	She sent him a note of thanks. 她寄给他一封简短的感谢信。
拓展词义	v. 记录，注意 n. 纸币，评注	A villager had noted the number of the truck. 一个村民记下了车牌号。 There ought to be a note on this obsolete word. 这个过时的词应有注释。

习惯用法	note down 把……记下

area [ˈɛəriə]		
核心词义	n. 地区，区域	People in cold areas live longer. 寒带地区的人寿命较长。
拓展词义	n. 面积，方面	What's the area of your garden? 你的花园有多大面积?

sign [sain]		
核心词义	n. 标记，符号，记号，指示牌	I'll be waiting for you at the entrance of the pub which has a sign painted with a red lobster. 我将在画着红龙虾招牌的酒吧门口等你。
拓展词义	n. 征兆，迹象 v. 签名（于），署名	He wants all of us to sign. 他希望我们都签名。
习惯用法	sign in 签到；签收 sign on/ up 签约受雇用	
联想词汇	signal [ˈsignl] n. 信号，导火线，动机，标志 　　　　　　　 v. 发信号，用信号通知	
词语辨析	signal 和 sign 都有信号、标号的意思。 signal 是指传递信息的、体现为特殊声音或动态模式的信号；而 sign 是指有特定意义的象征性符号、标记、有指示作用的标志物或者招牌。	

reminder [riˈmaində]	
核心词义	n. 提示牌　This has been a timely reminder of the need for constant care. 这件事适时地提醒我们要注意时时谨慎。

fail [feil]	
核心词义	v. 无视，忘记　When I wanted his help he failed me. 当我需要他帮助时，他却使我失望。

拓展词义	v. 失败，不及格	The teacher failed me in mathematics. 老师给我数学不及格。
习惯用法	fail of 缺乏……能力，不能达到 fail to 没有（做某事），疏忽，忘记（做某事）	

obey [əˈbei]

核心词义	v. 服从，听从	The boy won't obey. 这个孩子不听话。

17

Always young
青春常驻

appear [əˈpiə]

核心词义	*v*. 登场，扮演	They will appear on the stage. 他们一会儿就要登台演出了。
拓展词义	*v*. 出现，显得 发表，刊登	In my opinion, such chance won't appear again. 在我看来这样的机会恐怕永远不会再来。 His article appeared in China Daily yesterday. 他的文章昨天发表于《中国日报》上。
习惯用法	It appears to me that... 据我看来，我觉得…… It begins to appear that... 看起来似乎……	

stage [steidʒ]

核心词义	*n*. 阶段；舞台，舞台生涯	The moment the clown appeared on stage, the audience folded up. 小丑一出现在舞台上，观众们个个笑得前俯后仰。 He was suffering from cancer which had already reached an advanced stage. 他的癌症已经到晚期了。
拓展词义	*v*. 上演	That scene will not stage well. 那场戏不会演好。

bright [brait]

核心词义	a. 明亮的，鲜艳的；聪明的，生机勃勃的	My mother wears a bright yellow coat. 我妈妈穿着一件艳黄色的外套。Look at his bright face; he is not a bit old. 看他满面春风，一点儿也不老。
联想词汇	brilliant ['briljənt] a. 灿烂的，有才气的，杰出的	
词语辨析	bright, brilliant 含明亮的、发光的的意思。bright 比较普通，指明亮的；brilliant 意义比 bright 更强，表示光辉夺目的。	

stocking ['stɔkiŋ]

核心词义	n. 长袜（女用）	Something likes stocking is on the ground. 地上有像袜子一样的东西。

sock [sɔk]

核心词义	n. 短袜	There is a hole in my sock. 我的袜子上有个洞。

Lesson

18

He often does this!
他经常干这种事！

---

pub [pʌb]		
核心词义	*n*. 酒吧，小酒店	They've gone down to the pub for a drink. 他们到酒店喝酒去了。

landlord [ˈlændlɔːd]		
核心词义	*n*. 地主，房东；店主	He is the landlord of this pub. 他是这家酒店的店主。

bill [bil]		
核心词义	*n*. 账单，钞票，票据	His hotel bill comes to 20 pounds. 他的旅馆账款总共是 20 英镑。
拓展词义	*n*. 议案 *v*. 送交某人账单；贴广告	The bill was carried by the Senate. 这项法案获得参议院通过。 We'll bill you next week for your purchases. 下周我们将把你购买的物品开账单给你。

Lesson

19

Sold out
票已售完

Lesson 18 他经常

---

hurry [ˈhʌri]

核心词义	v. 催促，匆忙	Let's hurry a bit，we are far behind them. 咱们得快点，咱们比他们落后多了。
拓展词义	n. 匆忙，急忙	Don't drive so fast; there's no hurry. 不要开这么快，不必急急忙忙的。
习惯用法	hurry up 快，赶快 No hurry at all. 不用慌。	

ticket office

核心词义	售票处	My sister works in the ticket office. 我姐姐在售票处工作。

pity [ˈpiti]

核心词义	n. 遗憾，怜悯	It was a pity that the weather was so bad. 天气这样恶劣，真遗憾。

exclaim [iksˈkleim]

核心词义	v. 大叫，呼喊，大声叫	She exclaimed in delight when she saw the presents. 她见到礼品高兴得叫了起来。
习惯用法	exclaim against 强烈的不赞成 exclaim at 抗议	
词根词缀	词根-claim 表示喊、叫的含义，例如：acclaim [əˈkleim] v. 向……欢呼，向……喝彩；称赞	

return [ri'tə:n]

核心词义	vt. 归还，返回	He will return to London the week after next. 再下个星期他将返回伦敦。
拓展词义	n. 返回，回复，复发	I hope you will not have any return of your illness. 希望你的病不再复发。
习惯用法	in return（for）作为……的报答，交换 return to 回到（某个话题、某种状态），恢复	

sadly ['sædli]

核心词义	ad. 悲痛地，悲哀地，丧气地	She put down the phone, sighed, and shook her head sadly. 她放下电话，叹着气，悲哀地摇了摇头。

Lesson

20

One man in a boat
独坐孤舟

---

catch [kætʃ]

核心词义	*v*. (caught, caught) 捉住	Catch your hat! 抓住你的帽子！
拓展词义	*v*. 赶上（车、船等）	Quickly, otherwise we may not catch the train. 快点儿，否则我们就可能赶不上火车了。
习惯用法	catch up 抓起（某物），（被）卷入，赶上 catch up with 追上，赶上	
联想词汇	capture ['kæptʃə] *n*. 战利品，捕获之物 *v*. 抓取，俘虏，夺取	
词语辨析	catch，capture 含抓住、捕捉的意思。 catch 属于常用词，指通过追捕、机关或突然行动而提住在活动或躲藏中的人或物； capture 指通过武力或计谋战胜抵抗或困难而捕获某人或物。	

fisherman ['fiʃəmən]

核心词义	*n*. 渔民，钓鱼人	His father is a fisherman. 他的父亲是渔民。

boot [bu:t]

核心词义	*n*. 靴子	He laced up his boots. 他系紧靴子的鞋带。
拓展词义	*n*. 后备箱，行李箱	Put the luggage in the boot. 把行李放在汽车行李箱里。

waste [weist]

核心词义	n. 浪费；废弃物	We must combat extravagance and waste. 我们必须反对铺张浪费。
拓展词义	v. 浪费，使消耗；破坏 a. 废气的，无用的	The oil resources in some countries are rapidly wasting. 有些国家的石油资源正被迅速地消耗掉。 This is a waste and useless tyre. 这是个废弃无用的轮胎。

realize ['riəlaiz]

核心词义	v. 意识到，了解；实现	He realized his dream when he passed the entrance examination. 入学考试通过了，他的梦想就实现了。 If you were in the Sahara, you would realize the value of fresh water. 如果你在撒哈拉大沙漠，你就会知道淡水的价值了。
词根词缀	real 现实的 + 词缀-ize 使……	

Lesson

21

Mad or not?
是不是疯了?

---

mad [mæd]

核心词义	*a*. 发疯的；狂热的；恼火的	Don't fight with him, he is a mad man. 别跟他打架，他是疯子。 When the boss gets mad, leave him alone. 当老板生气时，不要理他。
习惯用法	be mad at 对……发怒	

reason ['ri:zn]

核心词义	*n*. 理由，原因	I can only guess the reason. 我只能猜测原因。
拓展词义	*n*. 理智，理性	His actions showed a lack of reason. 他的行动表明缺乏理智。
联想词汇	rational ['ræʃənl] *a*. 合理的，理性的	
词语辨析	rational，reasonable 含有理性的、合理的意思。 rational 强调有理性和思考、推理能力的； reasonable 指合情合理的、（价格）公平合理的。	

sum [sʌm]

核心词义	*n*. 量，总数，总和	The expenses came to an enormous sum. 开支总数巨大。
拓展词义	*v*. 合计，总结	Contributions summed into several thousand dollars. 捐款总数达数千美元。
习惯用法	sum up 总计；概括；总结	

determined [di'tə:mind]		
核心词义	a. 坚定的，下决心的	We have not got fully determined. 我们尚未完全决定。

22

A glass envelope
玻璃信封

dream [driːm]		
核心词义	v. 做梦，梦见	I dreamt about my teacher last night. 昨天夜里我梦见我的老师了。
拓展词义	n. 梦，梦想	I often return in dreams to my hometown. 我常常在梦中回到我的故乡。
习惯用法	dream of / about 梦见，梦想 设想，考虑	

age [eidʒ]		
核心词义	n. 年龄；老年；时代	They married at a late age. 他们年龄很大时才结婚。 The sage is the instructor of a hundred ages. 这位哲人是百代之师。
习惯用法	at the age of 在……岁时 for ages 很长的时间	

channel ['tʃænl]		
核心词义	n. 通道；频道；海峡	The ship passed the channel. 船驶过了海峡。

throw [θrəu]		
核心词义	v. (threw, thrown) 投，扔，抛，掷	Please do not throw litter. 请勿乱扔垃圾。

习惯用法	throw away 扔掉，浪费（金钱、时间等），错过（机会等） throw oneself at 猛然扑向，拼命讨好 throw oneself into 起劲工作 throw up 呕吐；向上抛

Lesson

23

A new house

新居

---

complete [kəmˈpliːt]

核心词义	*v.* 完成，使完整	When will you complete the task? 你什么时候完成任务？
拓展词义	*a.* 彻底的，完整的，已完成的	When will the work be complete? 这件工作什么时候完成？

modern [ˈmɔdən]

核心词义	*a.* 现代的，新式的，与以往不同的	He was steeped in modern history. 他埋头于近代史的研究。They went to an exhibition of modern art yesterday. 昨天，他们参观了现代美术展览。

strange [streindʒ]

核心词义	*a.* 陌生的，奇怪的	He stood in a strange street. 他站在一条陌生的街道上。
习惯用法	be strange at 对……显得外行	

district [ˈdistrikt]

核心词义	*n.* 区，地区，行政区	A number of unruly youths ganged up and terrorized the district. 一些不法青年结成一伙，使这个地区陷于恐怖。

Lesson

24

If could be worse
不幸中之万幸

manager ['mænidʒə]		
核心词义	*n.* 经理	Each department has its manager. 每个部门都有自己的部门经理。

upset [ʌp'set]		
核心词义	*a.* 不安的，烦乱的，不高兴的	He was very upset. 他非常心烦。
拓展词义	*v.* 推翻，扰乱，使心烦意乱	The news upset him emotionally. 这消息使他心烦意乱。

sympathetic [ˌsimpə'θetik]		
核心词义	*a.* 同情的；赞同的	He is a sympathetic person. 他是一个有同情心的人。
习惯用法	be /feel sympathetic to/towards... 对……表示同情；持赞同态度	

complain [kəm'plein]		
核心词义	*v.* 抱怨；控诉	I don't think I ever heard him complain of anything, but I knew how he felt. 我没有听到他抱怨过什么，但是我知道他内心的感受。
习惯用法	complain about 对某人或某物抱怨 complain of 抱怨；诉苦；抗议	

wicked ['wikid]

核心词义	a. 坏的，邪恶的	It's a wicked waste of money. 这样浪费金钱简直是罪恶。

contain [kən'tein]

核心词义	v. 包含，容纳	This book contains all the information you need. 这本书包含你所需的一切资料。
词根词缀	词根-tain 表示"保持"的意思。例如：attain [ə'tein] v. 达到，获得	

honesty ['ɔnisti]

核心词义	n. 诚实，正直	I am convinced in her honesty. 我为她的诚实所说服。
联想词汇	honor ['ɔnə(r)] n. 荣誉，头衔，尊敬 v. 尊敬，授予荣誉	

Do the English speak English?
英国人讲的是英语吗？

railway [ˈreilwei]	
核心词义	*n*. 铁路	The railway joins the two cities. 铁路把这两个城市连接起来了。

porter [ˈpɔːtə]	
核心词义	*n*. 搬运工人	The porter will carry your luggage to your room. 搬运工会把你的行李搬到你的房间去的。

several [ˈsevərəl]	
核心词义	*a*. 几个，若干	I go there several times each year. 我每年去那里几次。
拓展词义	Several of the children were in the garden. 有几个小孩在花园里。	

foreigner [ˈfɔrinə]	
核心词义	*n*. 外国人	I have never met a foreigner who speaks such perfect Chinese. 我从来没有遇到一个外国人汉语说得这么好。
词根词缀	foreign 外国的 + -er 人	

wonder [ˈwʌndə]	
核心词义	*v*. 感到奇怪	No wonder he is not hungry; he has been eating sweets all day. 难怪他不饿，他整天吃糖果。

拓展词义	*n.* 奇迹，惊奇，惊诧	He felt wonder mingled with awe at the Grand Canyon. 面对着大峡谷，他又惊奇又敬畏。
习惯用法	no wonder that 难怪，怪不得	

Lesson 26

The best art critics
最佳艺术评论家

art [ɑːt]		
核心词义	n. 艺术	She loves art. 她热爱艺术。
联想词汇	artificial [ˌɑːtiˈfiʃəl] a. 人造的，虚伪的 artistic [ɑːˈtistik] a. 艺术的	

critic [ˈkritik]		
核心词义	n. 批评家， 评论家	His work is highly thought of by the critics. 他的作品深受评论家推崇。
联想词汇	criticize [ˈkritisaiz] v. 批评，吹毛求疵	

paint [peint]		
核心词义	v. 画；上 漆，涂	The little girl paints nicely in watercolors. 小姑娘的水彩画画得很好。 He painted the wall green. 他把墙漆成绿色。
拓展词义	n. 油漆	Be careful with the wet paint. 小心，油漆未干。

pretend [priˈtend]		
核心词义	v. 假装	He pretended to be reading an important paper when the boss entered. 老板进来时，他假装在看一份重要的文件。
词根词缀	词根 pre-表示"在……之前"的含义 tend（词根）"伸展、倾向于、斗争、照顾"的含义。 例如：attend [əˈtend] v. 参加，注意，照料	

pattern [ˈpætən]

核心词义	n. 图案，式样，典范	She cut a pattern for her own coat. 她给自己的外衣剪了一个样子。
拓展词义	v. 模仿，仿制	They patterned a new machine. 他们仿制了一种新机器。
习惯用法	pattern sth. on 仿照……式样制	

curtain [ˈkəːtən]

核心词义	n. 窗帘；幕	The curtain was suddenly drawn and a bright light shone in. 突然窗帘拉了开来，一道强光照了进来。

material [məˈtiəriəl]

核心词义	n. 材料，原料；物质；资料，题材	Japan imports textile materials from Britain. 日本从英国进口纺织材料。During my three months' stay in the village, I collected enough material for two or three books. 我在村里待了三个月，搜集的材料足够写两三本书。
拓展词义	a. 物质的，重要的	The prosecution's case collapsed when a material witness failed to appear in court. 一名重要的证人没有出庭，因此诉讼辩论无法进行。

appreciate [əˈpriːʃieit]

核心词义	v. 欣赏，感激，赏识	We greatly appreciate your timely help. 我们十分感激你们及时的帮助。

notice [ˈnəutis]

核心词义	v. 注意，通知，留心	And you didn't notice anything unusual? 你觉察到什么异常的事情没有？

拓展词义	*n*. 注意，布告，通知	These rules are subject to change without notice. 这些规则可不经通知就进行更改。 Nobody took notice of the mischief of the matter. 没有人注意到这件事情所带来的危害。
习惯用法	take notice of 注意，留心 come to/into sb.'s notice 引起某人的注意 give notice of / that 通知……	

whether ['(h)weðə]

核心词义	*conj*. 是否；不管	Whether the football game will be played depends on the weather. 足球比赛是否举行将视天气而定。
习惯用法	whether... or... 是……还是……；或者……或者……；不是……就是…… whether or no/not 无论是不是；无论如何	

hang [hæŋ]

核心词义	*v*.（hung，hung）悬挂，吊	Hang your hat on the hook. 把帽子挂在衣钩上。
拓展词义	*v*. 居住，停留；绞死	He hangs out in an old house. 他住在一所旧房子里。 He was hanged for his crimes. 他因犯罪而被处绞刑。
习惯用法	hang up on sb. 挂断某人电话 hang on a minute 等一下	

critically ['kritikəli]

核心词义	*ad*. 批评性地	This must be examined critically. 这必须经过严格的检查。

upside down [ˌʌpsaid-'daun]

核心词义	上下颠倒地	He turns everything upside down. 他使每件事翻搅得乱七八糟。

A wet night
雨夜

tent [tent]		
核心词义	*n*. 帐篷	The children had a midnight feast in their tents. 孩子们半夜在帐篷里饱餐了一顿。
联想词汇	intent [in'tent] *n*. 意图，目的，意向 *a*. 专心的，决心的，热心的	

field [fiːld]		
核心词义	*n*. 田野，田地；（学习或研究的）领域	They are working in the field. 他们正在地里干活。 What are his main fields of interest? 他感兴趣的主要领域是什么？

smell [smel]		
核心词义	*v*. (smelled or smelt) 闻起来，嗅	The poor boy smelled the delicious odor of cooked meat. 这可怜的孩子闻到了香喷喷的肉味。
拓展词义	*n*. 味道，气味；嗅觉	There was a sweetish smell, vaguely reminiscent of coffee. 有一股甜甜的气味，使人隐隐觉得像是咖啡。 Dogs have a marvelous sense of smell. 狗有非常敏锐的嗅觉。

wonderful ['wʌndəful]		
核心词义	*a*. 极好的，精彩的	He told me a wonderful story. 他给我讲了个精彩的故事。

campfire ['kæmpfaiə]

核心词义	n. 营火，篝火	They damped down the campfire and then went to bed. 他们先将篝火封好，然后便去睡觉。

creep [kri:p]

核心词义	v. 爬行，匍匐	The dog crept under the car to hide. 狗爬到汽车下藏着。

sleeping bag ['sli:piŋ-bæg]

核心词义	睡袋	A good sleeping bag is an essential part of every camper's equipment. 一个好的睡袋是每个露宿者必不可少的装备。

comfortable ['kʌmfətəbl]

核心词义	a. 舒适的	Tom gratefully took in the comfortable sitting room. 汤姆感激地接受了那间舒适的起居室。
联想词汇	comfort ['kʌmfət] n. 舒适，安慰 v. 安慰	

soundly ['saundli]

核心词义	ad. 香甜地	The baby is sleeping soundly. 这孩子睡得很香。
拓展词义	ad. 完好地；健全地	He has been soundly defeated at chess. 他在国际象棋比赛中一败涂地。

leap [li:p]

核心词义	v. 跳，跳越，跳跃	Look before you leap. [谚] 三思而后行。
拓展词义	n. 跳跃，飞跃	He took a leap over an obstacle. 他跃过障碍物。
习惯用法	leap at 急切地抓住（机会等）	

| 词语辨析 | jump，leap 都含有跳、跃的意思。
jump 指从地面或其他立足点跳起来。
leap 常指跳过相当的距离，还含有连跑带跳的意味。 |

heavily [ˈhevili]

| 核心词义 | *ad*. 严重地，大量地 | His business is heavily in debt.
他的公司欠了很多债。 |

stream [striːm]

| 核心词义 | *n*. 小溪 | Can you jump across the stream?
你能跳过这条小溪吗？ |
| 拓展词义 | *n*. 流，股；潮流 | He hasn't the courage to go against the stream of public opinion. 他没有勇气逆舆论潮流行事。 |

form [fɔːm]

核心词义	*v*. 形成，组成，建立	Children should form good habits from the very beginning. 孩子们从一开始就应养成良好的习惯。
拓展词义	*n*. 形式，形状，表格	Ice, snow and steam are different forms of water. 冰、雪、蒸汽是水的不同形态。
习惯用法	form from 由……组成，用……构成 form into 组成……，编成…… in form 形式上 in the form of 以……的形式，呈……状态 fill in a form 填表格	

wind [wind]

| 核心词义 | *v*. (wound，wound) 蜿蜒
n. 风 | The road winds. 这条路弯弯曲曲。
A gentle wind disturbed the surface of the water. 微风拂动水面。 |

拓展词义	v. 上发条，缠绕	She is winding the wool. 她在缠毛线。
习惯用法	get one's wind 喘气 gone with the wind 破灭，化为泡影，不知去向 wind to a close 终止，结束	

right [rait]

核心词义	ad. 正好地，准确地，彻底地，向右，立即	Go right home at once, don't stop off anywhere on the way. 直接回家去，别在路上的什么地方呆下来。 I'm right behind you there. 我完全支持你。 I'll go right after lunch. 午饭后我马上去。
拓展词义	a. 对的，适当的，右边的，最恰当的 n. 正确，公正；权利；右边	I'll try to do whatever is right. 只要是正当的事，我都尽力去做。 She's the sort of woman who always says the right things. 她是一个说话总能恰到好处的女人。 We fought for the right of access to government information. 我们争取查看政府资料的权利。
习惯用法	all right 好，确实 by right of 凭借……（权利）；由于…… right away 立刻 right now 此时，刚刚	

Lesson
28

No parking
禁止停车

rare [rɛə]		
核心词义	*a.* 稀罕的，罕见的，珍贵的	It is a temple of rare architectural beauty. 论建筑之美，那是一座极少有的寺院。
拓展词义	*a.* 极好的；稀薄的	We have a rare old time at the party. 我们在聚会中尽情欢乐。

ancient ['einʃənt]		
核心词义	*a.* 古代的，古老的	We should read ancient authors. 我们应该读古代学者的著作。

myth [miθ]		
核心词义	*n.* 神话	Nobody believes in the myth about human beings becoming immortals. 谁也不相信人能成仙的神话。
联想词汇	mystery ['mistəri] *n.* 神秘	

trouble ['trʌbl]		
核心词义	*n.* 麻烦，困难；困境，动乱，纠纷	The old lady told me all her troubles. 这个老太太把她的烦恼都告诉了我。The trouble is that he doesn't have enough money. 麻烦在于他缺钱。
拓展词义	*v.* 使烦恼，使忧虑	I don't wish to trouble them. 我不愿意去麻烦他们。
习惯用法	be in troubles with 和……闹纠纷	

effect [iˈfekt]

核心词义	n. 结果，影响，效果	The advertising campaign didn't have much effect on sales. 这些广告攻势对销售额并没有起到多大作用。
拓展词义	v. 招致，引起	The temperature often effects a change of the state of matter. 温度常常引起物态的变化。
习惯用法	have an effect on 对……有影响；对……起作用 bring into effect 实行，实施，使生效，实现 take effect 开始实行；开始生效 in effect 实际上	
词根词缀	词根-fect 表示"影响"的含义。例如：affect [əˈfekt] v. 影响，作用	

Medusa [miˈdjuːzə]

核心词义	n. 美杜莎（古希腊神话中 3 位蛇发女怪之一）

Gorgon [ˈgɔːgən]

核心词义	n. 戈耳工（古希腊神话中 3 位蛇发女怪之一）（凡是见其貌者都会变成石头）

Lesson

29

Taxi!
出租汽车！

---

taxi [ˈtæksi]

核心词义	*n*. 计程车，出租汽车	Hi, taxi. 出租车停一下。
拓展词义	*v*. 用出租车送	All visitors have been safely taxied to the hotel. 所有的客人都由出租汽车安全地送到旅馆。

land [lænd]

核心词义	*v*. 着陆，下船，上岸	The spaceship landed safely. 宇宙飞船安全降落了。
拓展词义	*n*. 陆地，国土，土地	The storm blew over land and sea. 暴风雨在陆地上和海上呼啸。 There is a lot of good corn land around here. 这附近有许多良田。

plough [plau] = plow [plau]

核心词义	*v*. 用犁耕田	Farmers plough in autumn or spring. 农民在秋天或春天犁田。
拓展词义	*n*. 犁，耕地	Ploughs are pulled by tractors, or in some countries by oxen. 犁由拖拉机牵引，在一些国家则用牛来拉。

lonely [ˈləunli]

核心词义	*a*. 孤独的，寂寞的	She feels rather lonely in the strange town. 在这座陌生的城市里，她感到很寂寞。

联想词汇	alone [ə'ləun] *a*. 单独的，仅仅 lone [ləun] *a*. 孤单的，孤立的，单身的
词语辨析	alone，lonely，lone 含有孤独的意思。 alone 指独自一人的； lonely 指孤单的、孤独的； lone 用于诗歌中表示孤单的（感觉），指内心强烈的"忧愁"之感。

Welsh [welʃ]

核心词义	*a*. 威尔士的	One of my flatmates is a Welsh girl called Anna. 我有个舍友是威尔士的女孩子叫安娜。

roof [ruːf]

核心词义	*n*. 屋顶	The roof of the burning house fell in with a crash. 着火房子的屋顶哗啦一声塌下来。

block [blɔk]

核心词义	*n*. 街区；大块（木料、石料、金属等）障碍物；一幢大楼	There are road blocks on the country road. 乡间的马路上设有路障。 I live two blocks from the school. 我住在离学校两个路口的地方。
拓展词义	*v*. 堵，阻塞，阻碍	All the roads out of town had been blocked off by the police. 警察封锁住了所有出城的路。
习惯用法	block in 草拟 block off 封锁，封闭 block up 堵塞，挡住	

flat [flæt]

核心词义	*n*. 一套房间，公寓房	They divided the house into flats. 他们把那栋房屋分成许多套住房。

| 拓展词义 | *a.* 平坦的，扁平的；单调的 | We don't have flat land in this region. 我们这个地区没有平地。
It is a flat weekend.
这是个乏味的周末。 |

desert ['dezət]

| 核心词义 | *v.* 放弃，遗弃 | The baby's mother deserted him soon after giving birth. 那个母亲生下他后不久就把他遗弃了。 |
| 拓展词义 | *n.* [di'zə:t] 沙漠 | Vast areas of land have become desert. 大片的土地已变成沙漠。 |

Lesson

30

Football or polo?
足球还是水球？

polo ['pəuləu]		
核心词义	n. 水球	We watched a wonderful polo match. 我们看了一场精彩的水球比赛。

cut [kʌt]		
核心词义	v.（cut, cutting）切，割，砍	The paper cut my finger. 这纸割破了我的手指。
拓展词义	n. 伤口，切伤	That was a cut at me. 那是中伤我的话。
习惯用法	cut across 取捷径，走近路，超越 cut off 切断，隔绝，挡住，使电话中断 cut up 切碎，使痛苦，砍（割）伤	

row [rau]		
核心词义	v. 划（船）	Can you row me across the river? 你能划船将我送到河对岸吗?
拓展词义	n. 排，行 v. 吵架	The audience in the front rows made room for the late comers. 前排的观众为迟来的人让出座位。 She rowed the driver about the fare. 她为车费跟司机吵闹。
习惯用法	in a row 成一排	

kick [kik]		
核心词义	*v.* 踢	He kicked a penalty goal in the football match. 在这场足球赛中，他主罚，踢进了一个球。

towards [tə'wɔːdz]		
核心词义	*prep.* 朝，向	He headed towards the station. 他向车站赶去。
拓展词义	*prep.* 接近；为了；关于	The United Nations' work is towards peace. 联合国的工作是为了实现和平。 We arrived towards night. 我们接近半夜才到达。
联想词汇	ward [wɔːd] *n.* 守卫，监护，病房 *v.* 守护，监守	

nearly ['niəli]		
核心词义	*ad.* 几乎，差不多	He's only forty-one years old, and he has already been to nearly every country in the world. 他只有 41 岁，却几乎已经到过世界上的所有国家。
习惯用法	not nearly 绝不，相差甚远 pretty nearly 几乎，差不多	
词汇辨析	nearly, almost 虽然都可以表示几乎，但是当要表示接近或就要到了时最好用 nearly；当想表达不足或尚差一点儿时最好用 almost。	

sight [sait]		
核心词义	*n.* 景观，视力，眼界	I caught sight of an empty seat at the back of the bus. 我看到公共汽车的后面有一个空座位。
习惯用法	at first sight 一见就……，初次看见时 lose one's sight 失明 in sight 看得见 catch sight of 发现，看出	

Lesson

31

Success story
成功者的故事

retire [ri'taiə]		
核心词义	v. 退休，引退，撤退	He retired from the business when he was 60. 当他 60 岁的时候就退休了。

company ['kʌmpəni]		
核心词义	n. 公司	Which company do you work for? 你在哪个公司工作？
拓展词义	n. 陪伴，（一）群，（一）队	He fell in with bad company. 他交上了坏朋友。
习惯用法	in company（with）和……在一起 keep company with 和……常来往	

bicycle ['baisikl]		
核心词义	n. 自行车	He is learning to ride a bicycle. 他正在学习骑自行车。

save [seiv]		
核心词义	v. 挽救；积蓄；节省	If you save now，you will be able to buy a car soon. 如果你现在存钱的话，你不久就能买小汽车了。 I am going to take the bus to save money. 为了省钱，我打算乘公共汽车去。
习惯用法	save up 储存，储蓄 save for 除了……以外	

workshop [ˈwəːkʃɔp]		
核心词义	*n.* 车间	Smoking is out in the workshop. 车间里不准许吸烟。
拓展词义	*n.* 研讨会，讲习班	He'll chair a weekend workshop on politics. 他将主持一次周末政治研讨会。

helper [ˈhelpə]		
核心词义	*n.* 帮手，助手	The plumber's helper passes him tools. 水暖工的助手把工具递给他。

employ [imˈplɔi]		
核心词义	*v.* 雇佣	Our company employed about one hundred people. 我们公司雇用了大约100人。
联想词汇	employee [emplɔiˈiː] *n.* 雇员 employer [imˈplɔiə] *n.* 雇主	

grandson [ˈɡrændsʌn]		
核心词义	*n.* 孙子，外孙	They spoil their only grandson very much. 他们非常宠爱他们唯一的孙子。

Lesson

32

Shopping made easy
购物变得很方便

once [wʌns]		
核心词义	*ad*. 一次，曾经	I once went around the world. 我曾经周游过全球。
拓展词义	*conj*. 一旦…… 就……	Once you begin，you must continue. 一旦开了头，你就应当继续下去。
习惯用法	at once 立刻，马上 once again/ once more 再一次 once in a while 有时，间或，偶尔	

temptation [temp'teiʃən]		
核心词义	*n*. 诱惑，引诱	He was surrounded by temptations. 他受到各种诱惑。
联想词汇	tempt [tempt] *v*. 诱惑，怂恿某人做坏事	

article ['ɑːtikl]		
核心词义	*n*. 物品，东西	We should buy several articles at the shop. 我们在这家商场买点东西。
拓展词义	*n*. 文章；条款	This article allows no other explanation. 这项条款不容别的解释。

wrap [ræp]		
核心词义	*v*. 包，裹	The assistant wrapped the present up for her as quickly as possible. 这个店员以最快的速度为她把礼物包好。

习惯用法	be wrapped up in 包在……里，被……掩蔽 wrap up 包起来，裹起来

simply ['simpli]

核心词义	ad. 简单地，简直，仅仅	I have never met our new neighbors; I simply know them by sight. 我从未接触过我们的新邻居，只见过面。
联想词汇	simple ['simpl] a. 简单的，简朴的，单纯的 simplify ['simplifai] v. 简化，使简单	

arrest [ə'rest]

核心词义	v. 拘捕，拘留	Policemen have authority to arrest lawbreakers. 警察有权逮捕犯法者。
拓展词义	v. 制止，阻止	A driver uses brakes to arrest his car's speed. 司机用刹车降低车速。
习惯用法	arrest sb. for 因某事而逮捕某人	

Lesson

33

Out of darkness
冲出黑暗

darkness [ˈdɑːknis]		
核心词义	n. 黑暗，漆黑	The room was in darkness. 房间一片漆黑。

explain [iksˈplein]		
核心词义	v. 解释，说明	She explained her conduct to her boss. 她向老板说明了自己那种表现的原因。
习惯用法	explain sth. to sb. 向某人解释	
联想词汇	interpret [inˈtəːprit] v. 解释，翻译	
词语辨析	explain，interpret 含解释的意思。 explain 指解释不明的事情； interpret 侧重于用特殊的知识、判断、了解或想象去阐明特别难懂的事物。	

coast [kəust]		
核心词义	n. 海岸，海滨地区	Dalian is a town on the coast. 大连是沿海城市。

storm [stɔːm]		
核心词义	n. 暴风雨（雪）	The storm persisted for a week. 暴风雨持续了一个星期。

rock [rɔk]		
核心词义	n. 岩石，岩礁	The ship came close to the rocks and then sheered away. 这条船驶近岩礁，然后迅速转向避开。

| 拓展词义 | v. 使来回摆动；使震惊，使受震动 | The trees rocked in the wind. 树在风中摇摆。 |

shore [ʃɔː, ʃɔə]

| 核心词义 | n. 岸，滨 | There are lighthouses all along the eastern shore. 沿着东海岸都有灯塔。 |

light [lait]

| 核心词义 | n. 灯光，光亮，灯 | A dim light came from afar. 一缕暗淡的光线从远处射来。 |
| 拓展词义 | a. 轻的，光亮的，轻巧的，淡色的
v. 照亮，照明；点火，点燃 | The match lights easily. 这个火柴容易点燃。
This is a nice light room. 这是一间光线明亮的房间。
The conversation is light and gay. 谈话轻松愉快。 |

ahead [əˈhed]

| 核心词义 | ad. 向前地，胜于，在……前面 | Our company is ahead of other makers of spare parts for the airplane. 我们公司制造飞机零部件比别家的业绩好。 |
| 习惯用法 | ahead of 在……前头；早于；超过 | |

cliff [klif]

| 核心词义 | n. 悬崖，峭壁 | The narrow path zigzags up the cliff. 这条狭窄的小径曲曲折折地向峭壁伸延。 |

struggle [ˈstrʌgl]

| 核心词义 | v. 挣扎；拼搏 | The bandit struggled desperately. 那匪徒拼命挣扎。 |

拓展词义	n. 搏斗，战斗，奋斗	It was a hard struggle to get my work done in time. 为使工作按时完成，我做了一番努力。
习惯用法	struggle for 为……而斗争 struggle against（with）向……作斗争	

hospital ['hɔspitl]

核心词义	n. 医院	I see a hospital on my right hand. 我看到右侧有一所医院。

Lesson

34

Quick work
破案 "神速"

station [ˈsteiʃən]		
核心词义	*n.* （警察）局，车站，火车站	The radio station sets up an overseas broadcast program. 电台新设置了一个对外广播节目。 The railway station is some distance from the village. 火车站离这个村庄相当远。
拓展词义	*n.* 位置，地位	She is a woman of high station. 她是一位贵妇人。
习惯用法	railway station 火车站 a bus station 公共汽车站	

most [məust]		
核心词义	*ad.* 相当；非常	It was the most exciting holiday I've ever had. 那是我经历过的最令人兴奋的假日。
拓展词义	*a.* 最大的，最多的 *pron.* 大多数，大部分；最高，最大值	We spend most of March ploughing. 三月份的大部分时间我们都在春耕。 Peter made the most mistakes of all the class. 全班同学中，彼得出的错最多。

Lesson

35

Stop thief!
捉贼!

while [(h)wail]		
核心词义	*n.* 一段时间	It took a long while to do the work. 做这个工作花了许多时间。
拓展词义	*conj.* 在……期间，当……的时候；虽然	While I understand what you say, I can't agree with you. 虽然我理解你的意思，但我还是不同意。 While in prison, he wrote his first novel. 他在狱中写出了第一部小说。
习惯用法	after a while 不久，过一会	
联想词汇	meanwhile ['mi:nwail] *ad.* 同时 *n.* 期间	

regret [ri'gret]		
核心词义	*v.* 后悔，遗憾	I regret to tell you that my friend is ill. 我很遗憾的告诉你，我的朋友病了。
拓展词义	*n.* 遗憾，后悔，抱歉，失望	I have no regret about leaving. 我对离去一事毫不后悔。
习惯用法	It is to be regretted that... 令人遗憾的是…… regret to do sth. / regret doing sth. 遗憾做某事	

far [fɑ:]		
核心词义	*ad.* 遥远地，久远地，很，非常	This book is far different. 这本书很不一样。 He's fallen far behind in his work. 他的工作远远没有做完。

拓展词义	*a*. 远的，遥远的	I long to travel to far places. 我渴望去远方旅行。
习惯用法		as far as 就……；直到；到……为止 so far as 尽……说；就……而论 far from 远离；决非；决没有
词语辨析		far，remote 都含远的意思。 far 通常只指空间上的远距离，只有在 How far? 这句问话中，才可指远距离或近距离，间或也用以指时间上的距离； remote 遥远的，含有不易到达的意思。

rush [rʌʃ]

核心词义	*v*. 冲进，急忙；催促	Don't rush, take your time. 别急急忙忙的，慢慢来。 Don't rush me, I must think it over. 别催我，我要仔细想想。
拓展词义	*n*. 冲，奔；繁忙的活动	There was a mad rush to seats on the bus. 公共汽车上乘客疯狂地抢占着座位
习惯用法		rush out 仓促的跑出；赶着生产出 rush into 冲进，匆忙进入 rush off 仓促跑掉 rush up 催促

act [ækt]

核心词义	*v*. 行动；扮演；起作用	The time for thinking is past, we must now act. 思考的时间过去了，我们现在必须行动。 Oliver is acting tonight. 奥利弗今晚演出。
拓展词义	*n*. 行为，行动，法令	My first act was to run into the waiting room. 我的第一个行动就是跑进客厅。

习惯用法	act as 担任，充当；起……作用	
联想词汇	action [ˈækʃən] n. 动作，作用，战斗，行动，举动，行为，情节	

straight [streit]

核心词义	ad. 直接地，径直地；立即，马上	Let's go to the meeting straight away. 我们马上就开会去吧。
拓展词义	a. 直的，正直的，坦率的	There is a straight line under the sentence. 句子下面有一条直线。

fright [frait]

核心词义	n. 惊骇，害怕	A tree fell on the house and gave him a fright. 一棵树倒在房子上，吓了他一大跳。
联想词汇	frighten [ˈfraitn] v. 使惊吓，惊恐	

battered [ˈbætəd]

核心词义	a. 撞坏的；打扁了的	I'm going to replace my battered car with a fashion one. 我打算买辆时尚的汽车来取代我那辆破车。
联想词汇	batter [ˈbætə] n. 打击手	

shortly [ˈʃɔːtli]

核心词义	ad. 立刻，马上	She is shortly to leave for Mexico. 她很快要去墨西哥了。

afterwards [ˈɑːftəwədz]

核心词义	ad. 以后，后来	Soon afterwards he made his first public statement about the affair. 不久以后，他第一次就这一事件发表了公开声明。

Lesson

36

Across the channel
横渡海峡

record ['rekɔːd]		
核心词义	n. 记录；唱片；纪录	Some records of ancient civilization were discovered recently. 最近发现了一些古代文明的记录。 He broke a record in running. 他打破了一项赛跑的纪录。
拓展词义	v. 记录，将（声音等）录下	His voice does not record well. 他的声音录下来不好听。
习惯用法	keep a record (of) 记下来，记录	
词根词缀	词缀-cord 表示"中心"的含义	

strong [strɔŋ]		
核心词义	a. 强壮的，坚固的；坚强的；强烈的，深刻的	He is as strong as oxen. 他健壮如牛。 She has a very strong will. 她有着坚强的意志。
联想词汇	strength [streŋθ] n. 力量，力气，长处，强度	

swimmer ['swimə(r)]		
核心词义	n. 游泳者	The swimmer emerged from the lake. 游泳者浮出湖面。

succeed [sək'siːd]		
核心词义	vi. 成功，完成；继承，继任	The astronauts succeeded in returning from the moon to the earth. 宇航员们成功地从月球返回到地球。

习惯用法	succeed in 在……获得成功
	succeed sb. in 继承某人/接掌（某职权）
	succeed to 继承
联想词汇	success [sək'ses] n. 成功，成就
	successive [sək'sesiv] a. 接连的，连续的

train [trein]

核心词义	v. 训练，培养，锻炼	I am training for the Olympic Games. 我正在为奥运会训练。
拓展词义	n. 火车；一系列相关的事情或想法	Your telephone call interrupted my train of thought. 你的电话打断了我的思路。
习惯用法	by train 乘火车	

anxiously ['æŋkʃəsli]

核心词义	ad. 焦急地	They anxiously awaited the result. 他们焦急不安地等待着结果。

intend [in'tend]

核心词义	v. 打算；想要；计划	She intended that her daughter should study English. 她想让她的女儿学英语。
习惯用法	be intended to be 规定为……	
	intend for 打算供……使用	
	intend to do sth. 打算做某事	

solid ['sɔlid]

核心词义	a. 固体的，结实的，可靠的，硬的	Ice is water in a solid state. 冰是固态的水。 This old house has a very solid foundation. 这所旧房子有非常结实的地基。

Lesson

37

The Olympic Games
奥林匹克运动会

Olympic [əuˈlimpik]		
核心词义	a. 奥林匹克的	Winning an Olympic gold medal was, I suppose, the supreme moment of his life. 我认为荣获奥运会金牌是他一生中最重要的时刻。

hold [həuld]		
核心词义	v. (held，held) 举行，进行，召开	Our school will hold a debate this afternoon. 学校下午要举行一个辩论会。
拓展词义	n. 抓住，控制 v. 拿，握住；认为，相信；保持	She was holding a book (in her hand). 她（手里）拿着一本书。 The room can hold twenty people. 这屋子可容纳 20 个人。 Do you think the good weather can hold? 你认为好天气能持续下去吗？
习惯用法	hold back 阻碍；控制；保留 hold down 压住，使固定；控制，镇压 hold in 拿住，抱住 hold on 等一等 hold on to 坚持 hold up 举起，抬起，拿起，支持，忍受住	

government [ˈgʌvənmənt]

| 核心词义 | n. 政府 | Foreign governments have been consulted about this decision. 这一决定曾征询过外国政府的意见。 |

immense [iˈmens]

| 核心词义 | a. 巨大的, 广大的 | They made an immense improvement in English. 在英语方面他们取得了巨大的进步。 |
| 联想词汇 | immerse [iˈməːs] v. 使浸入, 使沉浸于 | |

stadium [ˈsteidiəm]

| 核心词义 | n. 体育场 | The stadium is being used for a match. 那个露天运动场正在进行一场比赛。 |

standard [ˈstændəd]

| 核心词义 | n. 标准, 规范 | The teacher sets high standard for his pupils. 这位老师给他的学生们定下高标准。 |

capital [ˈkæpitəl]

| 核心词义 | n. 首都, 资本, 大写字母 | The capital is located on the river. 首都位于河畔。 |
| 拓展词义 | a. 资本的, 主要的, 大写的 | We must develop capital market. 我们要发展资本市场。 |

fantastic [fænˈtæstik]

| 核心词义 | a. 巨大的, 极好的, 难以相信的, 奇异的 | We watched a fantastic play yesterday evening. 昨天晚上我们看了一场非常精彩的演出。 |

design [diˈzain]

| 核心词义 | v. 设计, 计划 | He designed us a beautiful house. 他为我们设计了一所很美的房子。 |

拓展词义	*n*. 设计，图样	The success of this car shows the importance of good design in helping to sell the product. 这种汽车的成功显示精良的设计对打开销路的重要性。
习惯用法	design for 计划；设计图	
联想词汇	sign [sain] *n*. 符号，手势，迹象 assign [əˈsain] *vt*. 分配，指派	

Lesson 38

Everything except the weather
唯独没有考虑天气

except [ik'sept]		
核心词义	*prep*. 除了……之外，若不是，除非	Everybody except me looks down upon him. 除了我以外人们都瞧不起他。
习惯用法	except for 除了……之外；只是…… except that 除了，只是	

complain [kəm'plein]		
核心词义	*v*. 抱怨	They complained bitterly about the injustice of the system. 他们愤恨地抱怨制度不公平。

continually [kən'tinjuəli]		
核心词义	*ad*. 不断地，频繁地	Why does he come here continually? 他为什么总是来这里呢？
联想词汇	continual [kən'tinjuəl] *a*. 不断的，频繁的 continuous [kən'tinjuəs] *a*. 连续的，继续的，连绵不断的	
词语辨析	continual，continuous，constant 含有连续的、不断的意思。 continual 指一段时间内多次发生、时断时续或中断时间很短而又接连发生； continuous 指连续不断的； constant 指始终如一的、不变的、持续地发生或反复地发生。	

bitterly [ˈbitəli]		
核心词义	*ad*. 刺骨地，伤心地；极其，非常	It is bitterly cold. 这天冷得刺骨。Her sister opposed it bitterly. 她姐姐强烈反对。
联想词汇	bitter [ˈbitə] *a*. 苦的，痛苦的 bit [bit] *n*. 一点儿，少量	

sunshine [ˈsʌnʃain]		
核心词义	*n*. 阳光	We lie in the sunshine for hours, getting a tan. 我们躺在日光下几个小时进行日光浴。

Lesson

39

Am I right?
我是否痊愈?

operation [ˌɔpəˈreiʃn]		
核心词义	n. 手术	The doctor advised an immediate operation. 医生建议马上开刀。
拓展词义	n. 行动，活动，操作	They were also given the opportunity to do some operation. 他们也有机会亲自去操作。
习惯用法	in operation 在活动（运转着）；实行着 bring into operation 实施，施行	

successful [səkˈsesful]		
核心词义	a. 成功的，如愿以偿的	She is a successful businesswoman. 她是一位很成功的女实业家。
词根词缀	success 成功 + ful ……的	

following [ˈfɔləuiŋ]		
核心词义	a. 下一个，其次的	Answer the following questions. 回答下列问题。
拓展词义	a. 下述的	The President has issued the following statement. 总统已经发表了下述声明。

patient [ˈpeiʃənt]		
核心词义	n. 病人	The patient was amused at the music. 听到音乐，病人感到快乐。
拓展词义	a. 有耐心的，能忍耐的	The young cashier gave a patient sigh. 年轻的出纳员忍耐地叹了一口气。

alone [ə'ləun]

核心词义	*a.* 单独的，独自的	He was alone in the house. 他独自一人在家里。
拓展词义	*ad.* 单独，独自	The key alone will open the door. 只有这把钥匙能开这个门。

exchange [iks'tʃeindʒ]

核心词义	*n.* 交换，汇兑，交易所	There have been numerous exchanges of views between the two governments. 两国政府间曾多次交换意见。
拓展词义	*v.* 交换，交易，兑换	We exchanged our opinions about the event at the meeting. 在会上，我们就此事交换了意见。
习惯用法	in exchange for 以……换	

inquire [in'kwaiə]

核心词义	*v.* 询问，问明，查究	The boss inquired of me concerning our work. 老板向我们了解我们工作的情况。
习惯用法	inquire sth. of sb. 向某人打听某事 inquire about 打听…… inquire after 问候 inquire into 调查，追究，了解	
词根词缀	词缀-quire 表示寻求、查找的含义。例如：acquire [ə'kwaiə] *vt.* 获得，取得，学到；require [ri'kwaiə] *vt.* 需要，要求	

certain ['sə:tən]

核心词义	*a.* 某个；一定的	A certain Mr. Brown telephoned while you were out. 你出去的时候，有个叫布朗的先生来过电话。 Are you certain that you'll get there in time? 你有把握及时赶到那里吗?

拓展词义	*pron.* 某几个，某些	Certain plants will not grow in this country. 有些植物在这个国家不能生长。
习惯用法	be certain of 确信，深信 be certain to 必然；一定 make certain of/ that 把……弄清楚，把……弄确实，保证	
词语辨析	sure，certain 都含确信的意思。 sure 强调主观上确信无疑的。 certain 指有充分根据或理由而相信的。	

caller [ˈkɔːlə]

核心词义	*n.* 打电话的人	This may help the authorities trace the caller. 这会对政府追查打电话者有帮助。

relative [ˈrelətiv]

核心词义	*n.* 亲戚，亲属	My uncle is my nearest relative. 叔叔是我最近的亲人。
拓展词义	*a.* 相对的，比较的	He retired and lived in relative isolation. 他退休后，生活比较孤寂。
联想词汇	relate [riˈleit] *v.* 讲，叙述；使联系，有关系	

Lesson

40

Food and talk
进餐和交流

hostess [ˈhəustis]		
核心词义	n. 女主人	I went away so my daughter acted as hostess. 那时我不在家，所以由我女儿招待客人。

unsmiling [ʌnˈsmailiŋ]		
核心词义	a. 不笑的，严肃的	The guards stood stiff-backed and unsmiling. 卫兵们挺直了腰站着，一笑不笑。

tight [tait]		
核心词义	a. 紧的；牢固的，紧身的，紧密的	She was wearing a tight dress. 她当时穿着紧身衣服。 I've got a very tight schedule today so I can't see you until tomorrow. 今天我的日程已经排得很满，所以明天才能见你。
联想词汇	loose [luːs] a. 宽松的，不牢固的，不精确的，随便的	

fix [fiks]		
核心词义	v. 凝视	Fix your eyes on the road and we will be much safer. 眼睛盯住公路，这样我们就更安全些。

拓展词义	v. 使……固定，修理，安装，安排	I will fix the same room for you. 我会给你安排同样的房间。 They know how to fix their cars. 他们知道怎样修理自己的汽车。
习惯用法	fix one's attention on/upon 集中注意力于…… fix up 修理；安顿，安排	

globe [ɡləub]

核心词义	n. 地球，地球仪，球体	There is plenty of water on the face of the globe. 地球表面有大量的水。

despair [dis'pεə]

核心词义	n. 绝望，失望	Defeat after defeat filled us with despair. 一次又一次的失败使我们完全绝望了。
习惯用法	in despair 绝望地 despair of 对……感到绝望，放弃……的希望	
联想词汇	desperate ['despərit] a. 不顾一切的，绝望的	

Lesson

41

Do you call that a hat?
你把那个叫帽子吗？

rude [ruːd]		
核心词义	a. 粗鲁的，无礼的	He was punished because he was rude to the policeman. 他因为对警察不礼貌而受了处罚。

mirror [ˈmirə]		
核心词义	n. 镜子	She was looking at herself in the mirror. 她正在照镜子。
拓展词义	n. 写照 v. 反映，反射	This is a mirror of times. 这是时代的反映。 The pond mirrors the surrounding trees. 那个池塘映出周围的树木。

hole [həul]		
核心词义	n. 孔，洞；裂口	He kicked a hole in the door. 他在门上踢了一个洞。

remark [riˈmɑːk]		
核心词义	v. 评论，注意，谈起	The editor remarked that article was well written. 编者评论说那篇文章写得很好。
拓展词义	n. 备注，评论，注意	In the light of his remarks, we rejected her offer. 鉴于他的评语，我们拒绝了她的提议。
习惯用法	remark on/upon 谈论，议论，评论	

remind [ri'maind]

核心词义	v. 使想起，提醒	The photo reminds me of my childhood. 这张照片使我想起了我的童年。
习惯用法	remind sb. of doing sth. 提醒某人想起某事 remind sb. of 使某人想起、记起…… remind sb. of sth. 提醒某人某事 remind sb. that 提醒	
词语辨析	remember，recall，remind 含记住、忆起的意思。 remember 属于常用词，指过去的事情仍在记忆中，不必费劲就能想起； recall 较 remember 正式，指对自己或他人的过去进行有意的回忆； remind 指由于受到提醒或启发而想起往事。	

lighthouse ['laithaus]

核心词义	n. 灯塔	The lighthouse flashes signals twice a minute. 灯塔每一分钟发出两次信号。

Lesson

42

Not very music
并非很懂音乐

musical ['mjuːzikəl]		
核心词义	a. 精通音乐的	She was from a musical family. 她出生于音乐世家。

market ['mɑːkit]		
核心词义	n. 市场，集市	She went to the market to sell what she had made. 她去市场出售自制品。
拓展词义	n. 销路	There is a good market for motorcars now. 现在汽车的销路挺好。

snake-charmer ['snik-ˌtʃɑːmə]		
核心词义	n. 玩蛇者（通常借音乐控制）	We noticed a snake-charmer with two large baskets at the other side of the square. 一会，我们注意广场的另一边有个带着两个大篮子的玩蛇者。
联想词汇	charmer ['tʃɑːmə] n. 魔术师	

pipe [paip]		
核心词义	n. 管子；烟斗；管乐器	He is playing a tune on his pipe. 他在用笛子吹奏一支曲子。
拓展词义	v. 以管输送，传送；用笛子吹奏	Nearly all the shops have piped music. 差不多所有的商店都连续播放音乐。 He piped so that we could dance. 他吹笛子伴奏好让我们跳舞。

tune [tjuːn]

核心词义	n. 曲调	The violin and the piano seem to be out of tune. 钢琴和小提琴好像不合调。
联想词汇	tone [təun] n. 音调，音质，语调	

glimpse [glimps]

核心词义	n. 一瞥，一闪	One glimpse at himself in the mirror was enough. 让他照着镜子看自己一眼就够了。
拓展词义	v. 瞥见	I glimpsed her among the crowd just now. 我刚才看到她在人群里。
习惯用法	glimpse of 瞥见，一瞥	

snake [sneik]

核心词义	n. 蛇	He was bitten by a poisonous snake. 他被毒蛇咬了。

movement ['muːvmənt]

核心词义	n. 运 动，动作，动向	We will enlist him in our movement. 我们要他参加我们的运动。 She watched the dancer and tried to copy her movements. 她观察那个跳舞的人，想模仿她的动作。

continue [kən'tinjuː]

核心词义	v. 继续，连续	The battle continued for several hours until darkness came on. 战斗持续了几个小时直到夜幕降临。

dance ['dɑːns]

核心词义	v. 跳舞	She began to dance as soon as she heard the music. 她一听到乐曲便跳起舞来。

拓展词义	*n*. 舞蹈，舞会，舞曲，舞步	We enjoyed ourselves at the dance party. 在舞会上我们玩得很愉快。 The band played a slow dance. 乐队奏起慢步舞曲。

obviously [ˈɔbviəsli]

核心词义	*ad*. 显然地	Your side has obviously gained by the change. 这一改变对你方显然有利。

difference [ˈdifərəns]

核心词义	*n*. 不同，差异；差距，分歧	It is both important and necessary to note this difference. 注意到这个差距是重要的和必要的。 There are many differences between living in a big city and living in the country. 生活在大城市与生活在乡村有许多不同之处。
联想词汇	differ [ˈdifə] *vi*. 不一致，不同 different [ˈdifrənt] *a*. 不同的 indifferent [inˈdifərənt] *a*. 漠不关心的，无重要性的，中立的	

Indian [ˈindjən]

核心词义	*n*. 印度人	These Indian guests are familiar with this book. 这些印度客人对这本书很熟悉。

Lesson

43

Over the South Pole
飞越南极

pole [pəul]		
核心词义	*n.*（地球的）极	The South and North Pole are the two points at opposite ends of the earth, about which it revolves. 南北极是地球绕之自转的两个相对的点。
拓展词义	*n.* 柱，杆（立在地面上或用来支撑的杆）；磁极，电极	We leaned the poles back against the wall. 我们把这些竿子斜倚在墙上。

flight [flait]		
核心词义	*n.* 飞行，飞机的航程，航班	The idea of flight had been kicking around for centuries before man actually achieved it. 在人们真正能上天飞行之前，飞行这种想法早已存在数百年了。

explorer [iks'plɔːrə, eks-]		
核心词义	*n.* 探险家，探测者，探测器	He is an adventurous explorer. 他是一个大胆的探险家。
联想词汇	explore [iks'plɔː] *v.* 探险，探测，探究	

lie [lai]		
核心词义	*v.*（lay，lain）躺着，位于	The factory lies to the west of town. 工厂位于城镇的西边。

拓展词义	v.（lied，lied）说谎 n. 谎话	He tried to tell me a lie about losing his wallet. 他试图使我相信他丢失了钱夹的谎言。
联想词汇	lay［lei］v.（laid，laid）放置，使躺下，使平息，产卵 lier［ˈlaiə］n. 埋伏者	

serious［ˈsiəriəs］

核心词义	a. 严肃的，严重的，危急的，认真的	Buying a house is a serious matter. 买房是一件需要认真考虑的事。 I want to have a serious talk with you. 我想要与你郑重其事地谈一谈。

point［pɔint］

核心词义	n. 地点，要点，尖端	Some of these points will have to be further elaborated as we go along. 这些要点中，有些我们在往下讨论时还得作进一步的详细阐述。
拓展词义	v. 指出，瞄准 n. 分数；意图	If you have a definite purpose in mind, get to the point promptly. 如果你心里有明确的意图，就干脆说出来。
习惯用法	point at 瞄准 point out 指出	
联想词汇	appoint［əˈpɔint］v. 任命，指定 disappoint［ˌdisəˈpɔint］vt. 使……失望	

seem［si:m］

核心词义	v. 像是，似乎	It seems as if it is going to snow. 看来天要下雪了。
习惯用法	It seems to me that 依我看……	
联想词汇	appear［əˈpiə］vi. 出现，显得	

| 词语辨析 | appear 和 seem 都含有看起来似……的意思。
appear 强调外表上给人某种印象，有时含有实质上并非如此的意思；
seem 表示有一定根据的判断，这种判断往往接近事实。 |

crash [kræʃ]

| 核心词义 | *v*. 坠毁，猛撞 | The plane crashed shortly after takeoff. 飞机起飞后不久便坠毁了。
The angry elephant crashed through the forest. 愤怒的大象闯过森林。 |
| 拓展词义 | *n*. 轰隆声，猛撞 | There was a serious car crash this morning. 今晨发生了一起严重的撞车事故。 |

sack [sæk]

| 核心词义 | *n*. 袋子；劫掠 | I bought three sacks of rice.
我买了三袋米。
The invaders put all to the sack.
入侵者把所有的东西洗劫一空。 |
| 拓展词义 | *v*. 装入袋中，洗劫 | They were sacking the potatoes in the field. 他们正在地里把土豆装袋。 |

clear [kliə]

| 核心词义 | *v*. 越过；澄清，清除障碍；放晴 | The horse No. 6 easily cleared every fence. 那匹 6 号马轻易地越过了各道栅栏。
Whose job is it to clear the accumulated rainwater from the streets? 清除街道上淤积的雨水是谁的工作？ |
| 拓展词义 | *a*. 无罪的；清楚的，明确的，清澈的 | He gave us a very clear explanation. 他给我们做了非常清楚的解释。 |

习惯用法	clear away 收拾干净；扫除；排除 clear up 整顿，清理，收拾，澄清 clear off 完成，清理，清算

aircraft ['eəkrɑːft]

核心词义	n. 飞机	All aircraft must fuel before a long flight. 所有飞机均需先加油方能作长途飞行。
联想词汇	craft [krɑːft] n. 工艺，手艺，飞船	

endless ['endlis]

核心词义	a. 无尽的，没完没了的	The child's endless crying has been wearing on my nerves all day. 那个孩子无休止的啼哭使我整天烦得要死。

plain [plein]

核心词义	n. 平原，草原	Animals range over the hills and plains. 动物在山丘和平原上出没。
拓展词义	a. 简单的，平坦的，平常的，单纯的	I'll tell you everything in plain words. 我将坦白地把一切事情告诉你。 She's in plain clothes. 她的穿着很朴素。

Lesson
44

Through the forest
穿过森林

forest ['fɒrist]		
核心词义	*n*. 森林	The traveler had to fight his way through the tropical forest with an axe. 探险者靠一把斧头奋力穿过热带雨林。

risk [risk]		
核心词义	*n*. 冒险，危险	They took a risk in driving on, notwithstanding the storm. 尽管有暴风雨，他们还是冒险驾车赶路。
拓展词义	*v*. 冒险	He risked his life when he saved the child from the fire. 他冒着生命危险把孩子从火中救出。
习惯用法	at the risk of 冒……之险；不顾……之风险	
词语辨析	danger，risk 都含危险的意思。 danger 系常用词，指目前的危险，也可指今后的或不一定发生的危险； risk 指风险，含有主动冒险的意思。	

picnic ['piknik]		
核心词义	*n*. 野餐	We had a picnic by the sea. 我们在海边搞了一次野餐。

edge [edʒ]		
核心词义	*n*. 边，边缘	The edge of the plate was blue. 这盘子的边是蓝色的。

strap [stræp]

核心词义	n. 带，皮带	I need a new watch strap. 我需要一条新表带。

possession [pə'zeʃən]

核心词义	n. 财产，所有，拥有；个人财产；领地，殖民地	The Egyptians strove with the Romans for the possession of the Nile Valley. 埃及人为占有尼罗河谷而与罗马人斗争。 She forsook her worldly possessions to devote herself to the church. 她抛弃世上的财物而献身教会。

breath [breθ]

核心词义	n. 呼吸，气息	We had to pause frequently for breath. 我们不得不经常停下来喘口气。
联想词汇	breathe [briːð] v. 呼吸	

content(s) [kən'tent]

核心词义	n.（常用复数）内有的物品；内容，容量	In my opinion the movie lacks contents. 依我看，这部电影缺乏实质性内容。
拓展词义	a. 满足的 v. 使满足	Now that she has apologized, I am content. 既然她已经道了歉，我也就满意了。 Simple praise is enough to content him. 简单的称赞就能使他满足了。

mend [mend]

核心词义	v. 修改，改进	It's never too late to mend. 改过不嫌迟。

Lesson
45

A clear conscience
问心无愧

---

clear [kliə]

核心词义	a. 无罪的，不亏心的	He had a clear conscience. 他问心无愧。

---

conscience ['kɔnʃəns]

核心词义	n. 良心	I had a guilty conscience about not telling her the truth. 我因为没有告诉她事实真相而感到内疚。
联想词汇	conscious ['kɔnʃəs] a. 神志清醒的，意识到的，自觉的	

---

wallet ['wɔlit]

核心词义	n. 皮夹，钱包	Someone has stolen my wallet from my back pocket. 有人从我的后口袋偷走了皮夹子。

---

savings ['seiviŋz]

核心词义	n. 存款	The old man kept his savings in the bank. 老人把他的储蓄存在银行里。

---

villager ['vilidʒə]

核心词义	n. 村民	So no other villager was more highly looked upon than him in the village. 所以在村里他可是个备受人尊敬的人。

percent [pə'sent]		
核心词义	百分之一，（与基数词连用）百分之……的	I am a hundred percent in agreement with you. 我百分之百同意你的看法。
联想词汇	per [pəː, pə] *prep*. 每，每一；依照，根据 percentage [pə'sentidʒ] *n*. 百分率	

Lesson

46

Expensive and uncomfortable
既昂贵又受罪

unload [ˌʌnˈləud]		
核心词义	v. 卸货；摆脱	John began to unload his trouble onto his mother. 约翰开始把他的烦恼告诉他的母亲。
习惯用法	unload one's mind 解除心中的焦虑	

wooden [ˈwudn]		
核心词义	a. 木头的	The floor was made of wooden blocks. 地板是用木块拼成的。
拓展词义	a. 僵硬的，呆板的	The actress gave a rather wooden performance. 那个女演员的表演相当呆板。

extremely [iksˈtriːmli]		
核心词义	ad. 极其，非常	I'm extremely grateful to you. 我非常感谢您。

occur [əˈkəː]		
核心词义	v. 出现，存在，发生	Don't let the mistake occur again. 不要让这种错误再次发生。
习惯用法	occur to 想起，想到 occur to sb. 使某人突然想到	

词语辨析	happen, chance, occur, take place 含发生的意思。 happen 为常用词语，指一切客观事物或情况的偶然或未能预见地发生； chance 指偶然发生、碰巧； occur 指按计划使某事发生，通常所指的时间和事件都比较确定； take place 指发生事先计划或预想到的事物。

astonish [əsˈtɔniʃ]

核心词义	v. 使……惊讶	He was astonished at what he found. 他发现的情况使他十分惊讶。
习惯用法	be astonished at sth. 对某事感到惊讶	

pile [pail]

核心词义	n. 堆	Collect the books and put them in a pile on my desk. 把书收起来放在我的桌子上。
拓展词义	v. 堆，堆积，拥挤	Cars often pile up here in the rush hours. 在交通高峰期汽车往往在这里挤成一团。
习惯用法	pile up 堆积；积聚	

woollen [ˈwulən]

核心词义	a. 羊毛的，羊毛制的，毛织的	She wears a woollen scarf. 她围着一条羊毛围巾。

goods [gudz]

核心词义	n. （常用复数）货物，商品	There're a large variety of goods in the shops. 商店里有各式各样的商品。

discover [disˈkʌvə]

核心词义	v. 发现，碰见	Columbus discovered America in 1492. 哥伦布于 1492 年发现了美洲。

拓展词义	v. 了解到	We'll discover who did it. 我们会查出是谁干的。
联想词汇	discovery [dis'kʌvəri] n. 发现（物）	
词根词缀	dis-去掉 + cover 盖子	

admit [əd'mit]

核心词义	v. 允许进入，承认	The rules and regulations admit of no other explanation. 这些规章制度不容许有其他解释。
习惯用法	admit sb. into/in 接纳某人进入……；吸收某人参加…… admit of 容许有；有……可能	
词根词缀	词根-mit 表示"做出，送出"的含义。例如：commit [kə'mit] v. 委托（托付），犯罪，承诺	
联想词汇	permit [pə(:)'mit] n. 许可证，执照 v. 允许，许可 submit [səb'mit] v. 呈送，递交；主张；使服从，屈服	

confine ['kɔnfain]

核心词义	v. 关在（一个狭小的空间里）	The thief was confined in a prison. 窃贼被关押在监狱里。
拓展词义	v. 限制	Please confine your remarks to the issues at hand. 请你把话题局限在手头的问题上。
习惯用法	be confined to（局）限于，（被）限制	
联想词汇	define [di'fain] vt. 定义，解释	

normal ['nɔːməl]

核心词义	a. 正常的，通常的；正规的	She braced herself to lead a normal life. 她振作起来去过正常生活。 He received four years of normal edication at college. 他在大学受了四年正规教育。
联想词汇	norm [nɔːm] n. 标准，规范 abnormal [æb'nɔːməl] a. 反常的，不正常的，不规则的	

Lesson 47

A thirsty ghost
嗜酒的鬼魂

thirsty [ˈθəːˌsti]		
核心词义	*a*. 贪杯的；口渴的	They watered the thirsty fields. 他们给干旱的土地灌水。

ghost [ɡəust]		
核心词义	*n*. 鬼，幽灵	Do you believe in ghosts? 你相信有鬼吗?

haunt [hɔːnt]		
核心词义	*v*. （鬼）来访，闹鬼	The old castle is said to be haunted. 这座古堡据说有鬼魂出没。
拓展词义	*v*. 常到，出没，萦绕于心	Memories of her childhood haunted her. 童年时代的记忆经常在她脑中萦绕。

block [blɔk]		
核心词义	*v*. 堵	They blocked the entrance with big stones. 他们用大石块堵住了入口。

furniture [ˈfəːnitʃə]		
核心词义	*n*. 家具	This old French table is a very valuable piece of furniture. 这张古老的法国餐桌是件很有价值的家具。

whiskey [ˈ(h)wiski]		
核心词义	*n*. 威士忌酒	Whiskey is best enjoyed after dinner. 威士忌最好在晚餐后享用。

suggest [sə'dʒest]

核心词义	v. 建议，提议；提醒，暗示	They accepted the paper and suggested only one change. 他们接受了这篇论文，只提出改动一个地方。 Her smile suggests her consent. 她的微笑意味着同意。
习惯用法	suggest that 提议；提出；建议	

shake [ʃeik]

核心词义	v. (shook，shaken) 摇动；握手；动摇	Shake up the salad-dressing before you put it on. 把色拉调味汁摇匀后再洒在色拉上。 Nothing can shake the basis for my belief. 什么也动摇不了我信念的基础。
拓展词义	n. 摇动，震动；哆嗦	Give the bottle a couple of shakes before pouring the juice. 倒果汁前先把瓶子摇动几下。
习惯用法	shake hands with 与……握手 shake off 撵走，摆脱；抖落 shake up 摇匀，使振作 be shaken at 被……惊吓	

accept [ək'sept]

核心词义	vt. 接受，同意，承担（责任等）	If you accept, please let me know. 如果你接受的话，请通知我。 The firm accepted personal cheques. 这家公司承兑私人支票。
习惯用法	accept... as /to be... 把……看作；认为……是	
词语辨析	receive，accept 都含收到、接受的意思。 receive 指收到，着重行为本身，而不涉及收受者是否接受； accept 指领受、接收，着重除行为本身以外，还表示接受者经过考虑以后愿意接受。	

Lesson

48

Did you want to tell me something?
你想对我说什么吗？

pull [pul]		
核心词义	v. 拉，拖，拔	I don't think the financial minister is popular enough to pull many votes at the next election. 我认为财政部长并不怎么受欢迎，他不会在下届大选中拉到许多选票。
拓展词义	n. 拉，拖；拉力，牵引力，引力	He gave a pull on the rope. 他拉了一下绳子。
习惯用法	pull apart 扯断，扯开 pull away 脱身，离开，（从危险中）逃脱 pull down 拉倒，摧毁，推翻；打倒，使（价格）下降 pull in（车）进站，停站；（船）靠岸 pull off 扯下；撕开，剥掉，脱（帽、衣等） pull out 拔出，挖出；突然撤走（车、船）驶出，度过难关 pull over 把……拉回来；（把……）划到岸边，（把……）开到路边 pull through（使）度过难关；使度过（危险等）；使恢复健康 pull together 合作，齐心协力；恢复……的团结 pull up 拔起；（使）停下；阻止	

cotton wool /ˌkɒtn-'wul/		
核心词义	n. 药棉	I tried to say something, but my mouth was full of cotton wool. 我想说点什么，但我嘴里塞满了药棉。

collect [kəˈlekt]		
核心词义	v. 收集，采集；聚集，征集	It's my hobby to collect stamps. 集邮是我的嗜好。 A crowd soon collected at the scene of the accident. 群众迅速聚集在事故现场。

collection [kəˈlekʃən]		
核心词义	n. 收藏品，收集物	The collection is housed in a fine building. 这批收藏品存放在一座漂亮的房子里。
拓展词义	n. 募集的款项，捐款；堆积物	His workmates made a collection for his leaving party. 他的同事为他的告别晚会募捐。 There is a collection of rubbish in the corner. 角落里有一堆垃圾。

nod [nɔd]		
核心词义	v. 点头，打盹，打瞌睡	She nodded to show that she agreed with me. 她点头表示同意我的意见。

meanwhile [ˈmiːnwail]		
核心词义	ad. 同时 n. 期间	They'll be here soon. Meanwhile we'll have some coffee. 他们即刻就到，我们现在先喝点儿咖啡。

Lesson

49

The end of a dream
美梦告终

tired [ˈtaiəd]		
核心词义	*a*. 疲劳的，累的，厌烦的	I'm tired of your words. 我听腻了你的话。
习惯用法	be tired of 对……不再感兴趣	

real [ˈriːəl]		
核心词义	*a*. 实际的，现实的，真正的，真实的	This is a real experience, not a dream. 这是一次真实的经历，并不是做梦。
联想词汇	reality [ri(ː)ˈæliti] *n*. 现实，实际，真实	

owner [ˈəunə]		
核心词义	*n*. 主人，所有人，物主	Do you know the name of the owner? 你知道主人的名字吗？
联想词汇	owe [əu] *vt*. 欠（债等），归功于，应感谢 own [əun] *a*. 自己的 *vi*. 承认，拥有	

spring [spriŋ]		
核心词义	*n*. 春季，春天；弹簧	Trees put forth buds and leaves in spring. 树木在春天发芽长叶。

mattress [ˈmætris]		
核心词义	*n*. 床垫	Constance doesn't like white mattress. 康斯坦斯不喜欢白床垫。

gust [gʌst]		
核心词义	*n.* 一阵风	A gust of wind blew the front door shut. 一阵大风吹来，把前门关上了。
联想词汇	guest [gest] *n.* 客	

sweep [swiːp]		
核心词义	*v.*（swept, swept）扫，刮	Many villages were swept away by the flood. 洪水冲走了很多村庄。
拓展词义	*n.* 打扫，清扫	This floor needs a good sweep. 这地板需要好好清扫一下。
习惯用法	sweep away 扫清，迅速消灭，冲走 sweep up 打扫干净，收拾干净 sweep over 风靡，向……扩展	

courtyard [ˈkɔːtjɑːd]		
核心词义	*n.* 庭院，院子	This gate leads into the courtyard. 这扇门通向院子。

smash [smæʃ]		
核心词义	*n.* 破碎，摔碎；猛击，猛撞	We heard the smash of plates breaking in the kitchen. 我们听到厨房里盘子破碎的声音。 He gave me a smash on my head. 他猛击我的头部。
拓展词义	*v.* 粉碎，摔碎，溃裂	Some kids smashed her bedroom window. 一些小孩打碎了她卧室的玻璃。
习惯用法	smash up 捣碎；摔碎 smash into 碰撞；猛冲	

miraculously [mi'rækjuləsli]

核心词义	*ad*. 奇迹般地	It was a terrible explosion, but, miraculously, no one was killed. 这是一次可怕的爆炸，但是没有一个人死亡，真是奇迹。

unhurt ['ʌn'həːt]

核心词义	*a*. 没有受伤的	I thought he was really unhurt but he was faking. 我原以为他真的没有受伤，不料他只是在佯装没受伤而已。
联想词汇	hurt [həːt] *v*. 伤害，（使）疼痛；对……有害 *n*. 肉体上的伤痛；精神上的创伤	
词语辨析	hurt, wound, injure 都含有使受伤、伤害的意思。 hurt 表示身体受伤，口语化，也可以表示情感受伤害； wound 是指枪伤或者其他利器所导致的伤； injure 表示身体受伤、某人的事业受损、名誉受到伤害，或使某人受到冤枉或委屈。	

glance [glɑːns]

核心词义	*v*. 扫视，匆匆一看，一瞥	He glanced at his watch and then looked at the sky. 他看了看手表，然后又看了看天空。
习惯用法	at a glance 看一眼，乍一看 glance over 浏览，粗略地阅读	

promptly ['prɔmptli]

核心词义	*ad*. 敏捷地，迅速地	He paid the money back promptly. 他很快就把钱还了。

Lesson

50

Taken for a ride
乘车兜风

ride [raid]		
核心词义	*n*. 旅行；乘坐，乘车	I had a ride on a horse for an hour. 我骑马骑了一个小时。
拓展词义	*v*. (rode, ridden) 乘，骑	She is riding a bicycle. 她正在骑一辆自行车。
习惯用法	ride in/on 乘车	

excursion [iks'kə:ʃən]		
核心词义	*n*. 远足，游览，参观	Our class will make an excursion to the seaside. 我们班将去海边旅行。
联想词汇	expedition [ˌekspi'diʃən] *n*. 探险，远征 voyage ['vɔiidʒ] *n*. 航行，旅程 trip [trip] *n*. 旅行；远足	
词语辨析	journey, trip, excursion, voyage, expedition 都含旅行的意思。 journey 应用范围很广，指有预定地点的陆上、水上或空中的单程长、短途旅行，一般来说，它着重指长距离的陆上的旅行； trip 为一般用语，指任何方式的，从事业务或游览的旅行，往往着重于短途旅行； excursion 指娱乐性的短途旅行； voyage 主要指乘船作水上旅行； expedition 指远征、探险、考察等。	

conductor [kənˈdʌktə]		
核心词义	n. 售票员	The bus conductor collected money from the passengers. 公共汽车售票员向乘客收钱。
拓展词义	n. 导体	Copper is a good conductor of heat. 铜是热的良导体。

view [vjuː]		
核心词义	n. 视野，风景，见解，观察，观看，认为	In view of our long-standing relationship, we agree to allow you a discount. 考虑到我们长期的关系，我方同意给你方折扣。 I'll sit here and look at the view. 我要坐在这里观看景色。
拓展词义	v. 看，考虑，认为	We can view the problem in many ways. 我们可以从多方面来考虑这个问题。
习惯用法	in view of 鉴于；考虑到 with the view of 为……的目的 in one's view 依照个人的见解	

Lesson

51

Reward for virtue
对美德的奖赏

reward [ri'wɔːd]		
核心词义	*n*. 报酬，酬谢，赏金	He will expect some reward after working so hard. 他工作很努力，会得到报偿的。
拓展词义	*v*. 奖赏，酬谢	How can I reward your kindness? 我怎样才能报答你的好心呢?
联想词汇	award [ə'wɔːd] *n*. 奖，奖品 *vt*. 授予，给予	
习惯用法	reward sb. for sth. 为某事报答某人 reward sb. with... for sth. 为某事而以……报答某人 in reward of 为酬答……；作为奖励	

virtue [ˈvəːtjuː]		
核心词义	*n*. 美德，优点	Among her many virtues are loyalty, courage, and truthfulness. 她有许多的美德，如忠诚、勇敢和诚实。

diet [ˈdaiət]		
核心词义	*n*. 日常饮食；节食	No sugar in my coffee, please; I'm dieting. 请不要给我的咖啡放糖，我在节食。
习惯用法	go on a diet 节食	

forbid [fə'bid]		
核心词义	*v*. (forbade, forbidden) 禁止，不准	The doctor forbids him smoking and drinking. 医生禁止他抽烟、喝酒。

词语辨析	forbid，ban，prohibit 都含禁止的意思。 forbid 系常用词，指命令某人不做某事。 ban 语气较重，指权威机关正式禁止，含严厉谴责之意，只能用事物作其宾语。 prohibit 指通过法律或政府法令禁止。

hurriedly ['hʌridli]

核心词义	ad. 匆忙地	He pressed on still more hurriedly. 他更加匆忙地往前赶。

embarrass [im'bærəs]

核心词义	v. 使……困窘，使……局促不安	She seems embarrass at the request. 她对于这个请求似乎感到难为情。

guiltily ['giltili]

核心词义	ad. 内疚地	He smiled guiltily and then put the parcel on the desk. 他内疚地笑笑，然后把那个包放到书桌上。

strict [strikt]

核心词义	a. 严格的，精确的	Our teacher is strict; we have to do what she says. 我们的老师很严格，我们不得不按她说的去做。

occasionally [ə'keiʒənəli]

核心词义	ad. 偶尔地	He occasionally writes to me. 他偶尔写信给我。
联想词汇	occasion [ə'keiʒən] n. 场合，机会，理由 case [keis] n. 情形，情况，箱子，案例	

Lesson

52

A pretty carpet
漂亮的地毯

temporarily [ˈtempərərili]		
核心词义	*ad* . 暂时地，临时地	Family is staying with me temporarily. 家人暂时过来住住。
联想词汇	temper [ˈtempə] *n* . 脾气，特征，趋向 contemporary [kənˈtempərəri] *n* . 同时代的人 *a* . 同时代的，属于同一时期的	

inch [intʃ]		
核心词义	*n* . 英寸（度量单位）	He missed the target by an inch. 他差一英寸就中靶了。

space [speis]		
核心词义	*n* . 空间，距离，空地，场所，太空，空白处	Keep some space between you and the car ahead. 跟前面的汽车保持一定距离。 Please write your name in the blank space at the top of the page. 请把姓名写在这页上面的空白处。
拓展词义	*v* . 把……分隔开	Space the chairs so that there is room for people to walk between them. 把椅子间隔摆放，以便人们从中走过。
联想词汇	cyberspace [ˈsaibəspeis] *n* . 信息空间 interspace [ˈintəˈspeis] *n* . 空间，中间，空隙 *vt* . 留……的间隔，留空隙	

actually [ˈæktʃuəli]		
核心词义	*ad* . 实际上，确实	Actually it's we that owe you a lot. 实际上，应该是我们感谢您。
联想词汇	virtual [ˈvɜːtjuəl] *a* . 实际上的，实质的	

Lesson

53

Hot snake
触电的蛇

hot [hɔt]		
核心词义	a. 充电的，带电的	Look out! There is a hot wire in front of you! 注意，你前面的电线带电。
拓展词义	a. 热的，热情的，辣的，棘手的	Hot words were exchanged between the two men. 两人之间激烈争吵起来。 A blast of hot air blows in. 一股热气吹进来。

fireman ['faiəmən]		
核心词义	n. 消防队员	I saw a fireman racing to the fire. 我看见一个消防队员冲入了火中。

cause [kɔːz]		
核心词义	v. 引起 n. 原因	We have achieved great successes in the cause of building up our country. 我们在国家的建设事业上取得了巨大的成就。 The child's headache may be caused by stress. 那孩子的头痛可能是紧张引起的。
习惯用法	in the cause of 为了…… have cause for 有理由……	
联想词汇	accuse [ə'kjuːz] vt. 责备，控告 excuse [iks'kjuːz] vt. 原谅，宽恕；使免除 　　　　　　　　　n. 理由，借口，原谅，道歉	

词语辨析	cause，reason 都含原因的意思。 cause 指产生结果的原因或使某事发生的原因； reason 指根据事实、情况或产生的结果，推导出结论的理由或道理。

examine [ig'zæmin]

核心词义	v. 检查，调查；考试，对……进行考核	The doctor examined the wound. 医生检查了伤口。 All candidates must first be orally examined. 所有的考生必须先参加口试。

accidentally [ˌæksi'dəntli]

核心词义	ad. 偶然地，意外地	We accidentally broke the radio. 我们不小心弄坏了收音机。

reminds [ri'maindz]

核心词义	n. 尸体，残骸	There were a lot of remiands of fish on the sea. 海上有很多鱼的残骸。
联想词汇	remind [ri'maind] vt. 使想起，提醒	

wire ['waiə]

核心词义	n. 电线，电报，金属丝	Electricity is carried along wires. 电沿着电线传导。

volt [vəult]

核心词义	n. 伏特	We converted from 220 to 110 Volt. 我们从 220 伏特转换成 110 伏特。
联想词汇	voltage ['vəultidʒ] n. 电压 revolt [ri'vəult] vi. 叛乱，反抗，起义	

power line

核心词义	电力线	Keep away from the high-tension power line. 勿靠近高压电线。

solve [sɒlv]

核心词义	v. 解答，解决	He finally solved the difficulty of transportation. 他终于解决了运输的困难。
联想词汇	resolve [ri'zɒlv] v. 决定，解决，决心 dissolve [di'zɒlv] v. 溶解，解散	

mystery ['mistəri]

核心词义	n. 神秘，神秘的事物	The flying saucer is yet an unsolved mystery. 飞碟仍然是未解之谜。

snatch [snætʃ]

核心词义	vt. 伸手去拿；抓住，迅速获得	We must learn to snatch at every chance. 我们必须学会抓住一切的机会。
拓展词义	n. 抢，夺；片段，短时间	The thief snatched her handbag and ran. 盗贼抢了她的手提包就跑。

spark [spɑːk]

核心词义	n. 电火花，火星	A single spark can start a prairie fire. 星星之火，可以燎原。
拓展词义	v. 发出火花 n. 略微，一点点	Fireflies sparked in the darkness. 萤火虫在黑暗中发光。
习惯用法	not a spark of 毫无，一点都不	
联想词汇	sparkle ['spɑːkl] v. 闪耀，冒火花	

Lesson 54

Sticky fingers
粘糊的手指

sticky ['stiki]		
核心词义	a. 粘的，粘性的	This floor is sticky; it needs cleaning. 这地板粘粘的；它需要清洗一下。

finger ['fiŋgə]		
核心词义	n. 手指	There are five fingers on each hand. 每只手有五个手指。

pie [pai]		
核心词义	n. 馅饼	Would you like some apple pie for dessert? 你想不想要些苹果派当甜点？

mix [miks]		
核心词义	v. 混合，弄混	Never mix water with chocolate. 千万别把水和巧克力混在一起。
拓展词义	n. 混合物，混乱	His first reaction was a strange mix of joy and anger. 他的第一反应很奇怪，高兴和愤怒掺杂在一起。
习惯用法	mix up 混合，掺合 mix with 与……混合	
联想词汇	mixture ['mikstʃə] n. 混合，混合物	

pastry ['peistri]		
核心词义	n. 面糊	You may flour the pastry board so that the dough doesn't stick to it. 你可以在做糕点的面板上撒些面粉，这样揉好的面粉就不会粘到板上了。

annoying [ə'nɔiiŋ]		
核心词义	*a*. 恼人的，讨厌的	He may be naughty and annoying, but he is a good boy for all that. 尽管他淘气又惹人讨厌，他还是一个好孩子。

receiver [ri'siːvə]		
核心词义	*n*. 电话的话筒，接收器；收款员；接待者	He hung up the receiver and went out. 他挂上电话听筒走了出去。

dismay [dis'mei]		
核心词义	*v*. 使……惊愕，失望，泄气	He was dismayed at his lack of understanding. 他对自己的无知感到沮丧。
拓展词义	*n*. 惊愕，气馁	I am filled with dismay at the news. 我对这个消息极为震惊。

recognize ['rekəgnaiz]		
核心词义	*v*. 认出，认可，承认	I can recognize his voice easily. 我很容易就听出他的声音来了。

persuade [pə'sweid]		
核心词义	*v*. 劝说，说服	I wish you could persuade her to think so. 但愿你能说服她去这样想。
习惯用法	persuade sb. to do sth. = persuade sb. into doing sth. 劝说某人干某事	

mess [mes]		
核心词义	*n*. 乱七八糟	There's a lot of mess to clear up. 有许多脏东西要清理。
拓展词义	*v*. 弄脏，弄乱	Stop messing about and listen to me. 别再胡闹了，听我说。

习惯用法	in a mess 零乱；肮脏
联想词汇	mission [ˈmiʃən] n. 任务，代表团，使命

doorknob [ˈdɔːnɔb]

核心词义	n. 门把手	String this note on the front doorknob. 把这张字条子挂在前门的把手上。

sign [sain]

核心词义	v. 签名（于），署名	He wants all of us to sign. 他要我们大家都签字。

register [ˈredʒistə]

核心词义	v. 记录，登记，注册，挂号邮寄	An increasing number of students are registering for degree courses each year. 每年，越来越多的学生注册学习学位课程。

Lesson

55

Not a gold mine
并非金矿

---

gold [gəuld]

核心词义	*n*. 金子，黄金；金色	Gold is found in rocks and streams. 黄金蕴藏在岩石与溪流中。
拓展词义	*a*. 金色的，金制的	Some gold coins were dug out from the ground. 几枚金币从地下挖了出来。

mine [main]

核心词义	*n*. 地雷，矿，矿山	The inspector went down the mine. 监察员已下到矿井里了。
拓展词义	*pron*. 我的	That's your coat; mine is here. 那是你的上衣，我的在这儿。
联想词汇	undermine [ˌʌndəˈmain] *vt*. 渐渐破坏，逐渐削弱 mineral [ˈminərəl] *n*. 矿物，矿石	

treasure [ˈtreʒəl]

核心词义	*n*. 宝物，财富	The museum has many art treasures. 这家博物馆收藏了很多艺术珍品。
拓展词义	*v*. 重视，珍惜	I certainly treasure the friendship between us very much. 我当然非常珍视我们之间的友谊。

revealer [riˈviːlə]

核心词义	*n*. 探测器	Many people are confident that 'The Revealer' may reveal something of value fairly soon. 很多人都相信那个"探测器"很快就能探测到一些有价值的东西。
联想词汇	reveal [riˈviːl] *vt*. 显示，透露	

detect [di'tekt]

核心词义	v. 发现，发觉，查明	He was detected in the act of stealing. 他在偷窃时被当场发现。
习惯用法	detect sb. in (doing)... 发觉某人在做（坏事）	

bury ['beri]

核心词义	v. 埋葬，隐藏，沉溺于	Whenever he is free, he will bury himself in a book. 只要他一有时间，他就埋头读书。
习惯用法	bury (oneself) in 埋头于；专心于	

cave [keiv]

核心词义	n. 山洞，洞穴	He concealed himself in a cave. 他把自己隐蔽在一个洞穴里。

seashore ['si:ʃɔ:]

核心词义	n. 海岸，海滨	As we walked along the seashore we saw lots of tiny crabs. 我们在海岸上散步时看到很多小蟹。

pirate ['paiərit]

核心词义	n. 海盗	The sailor suddenly saw a pirate jumping onto the deck. 那水手忽然看到一名海盗跳上了甲板。
拓展词义	n. 盗版 v. 剽窃，非法翻印	The sale of pirate record have is ban. 盗版唱片被禁止出售。

arm [ɑːm]

核心词义	v. 把……武装起来	War is certain, we should arm without delay. 战争肯定要发生，我们必须立即武装起来。

拓展词义	n. 手臂，袖子；武器	People were up in arms against the invaders. 人民拿起武器反抗侵略者。
习惯用法	armed with 用……武装起来	
联想词汇	alarm [əˈlɑːm] n. 警报，警钟 v. 警告，使惊慌	

soil [sɔil]

核心词义	n. 泥土，土地，土壤	Plants get the nutrition from the soil in which they grow. 植物从它们赖以生存的土壤中吸收养分。

entrance [ˈentrəns]

核心词义	n. 入口；进入；入学，登场	The car waited at the front entrance. 汽车在前门口等候。 The singer's entrance was greeted with applause. 那位歌星在掌声中登场。
联想词汇	enter [ˈentə] v. 进入，参加，登入	

finally [ˈfainəli]

核心词义	ad. 最后，最终	It's not finally settled yet. 这事还没有最后解决。

worthless [ˈwəːθlis]

核心词义	a. 毫无价值的，无用的	Don't read worthless books. 不要读没有用的书。
联想词汇	worthy [ˈwəːði] a. 应得某物，值得做某事 worth [wəːθ] n. 价值 a. 值多少，值得	

thoroughly [ˈθʌrəli]

核心词义	ad. 彻底地	He felt thoroughly broken down. 他觉得身体彻底垮了。
联想词汇	through [θruː] prep. 遍及；（时间）在……期间，从一端到另一端；经历；凭借；（原因）因为，由于 ad. 通过，过去 throughout [θruː(ˈ)aut] prep. 遍及，贯穿；在……期间	

trunk [trʌŋk]

核心词义	*n*.（汽车后部）行李箱	Let me take them to the trunk. 让我把他们放到后备箱吧。
拓展词义	*n*. 树干，躯干，象鼻	The boy could be seen with his legs wrapped around the trunk. 只见那男孩双腿盘着树干。

confident ['kɔnfidənt]

核心词义	*a*. 确信的，自信的	We need a confident leader to overcome these difficulties. 我们需要一个有信心的领导者来克服这些困难。
词语辨析	sure，certain，confident 都含确信的意思。 sure 强调主观上确信无疑的； certain 指有充分根据或理由而相信的； confident 强调对某人（物）坚信的或满怀信心的。	

value ['vælju:]

核心词义	*n*. 价值，重要性；价值观，价值标准	The expert set a value of 10,000 dollars on the painting. 专家给这幅画定价 1 万美元。 Our values and behaviour patterns are different from yours. 我们的价值观念和行为模式与你们的不同。
拓展词义	*v*. 评价，估价，重视	I valued the bike at 200 dollars. 我估计这辆自行车值 200 美元。
词语辨析	merit，value，worth 含优点、价值的意思。 merit 指成就或品质中值得赞扬的优点； value 指重要性、价值； worth 着重指人或物本质中的优点或价值。	

Lesson

56

Faster than sound!
比声音还快!

---

sound [saund]

核心词义	*n*. 声音，播音 *v*. 使发出声音； 发出信号	Sound travels slower than light. 声音传播比光慢。 She sounded a note of danger. 她发出危险的信号。
拓展词义	*a*. 健全的，完 好的，明智 的，正确的	That's very sound advice; you should take it. 那是非常明智的忠告，你应当接受。 The child has a sound mind in a sound body. 这孩子身心健康。

---

excitement [ik'saitmənt]

核心词义	*n*. 激动，兴奋	Very great excitement prevails throughout the country. 全国到处洋溢着极度兴奋的情绪。
拓展词义	*n*. 令人激动的事	Life will seem very quiet after the excitements of our holiday. 假期一阵兴奋后，生活会显得很平静。
词根词缀	excite 兴奋，激动 + -ment 名词后缀	

---

handsome ['hænsəm]

核心词义	*a*. 英俊的；漂 亮的	He looked tall, handsome and healthy. 他看上去高大、英俊、健壮。

Rolls-Royce [ˈrəulz-ˈrɔis]

核心词义	罗尔斯—罗伊斯	Rolls-Royce has produced a new model. 罗尔斯—罗伊斯公司已生产了一种新的轿车式样。
联想词汇	BMW 宝马 Audi 奥迪 Porsche 保时捷 Chrysler 克莱斯勒 Buick 别克 Lincoln continental 林肯大陆 Lexus 凌志 Honda 本田 Ferrat 法拉利 Hyundai 现代	Benz 奔驰 Volkswagonwerk（德文）大众 Chevrolet 雪弗莱 Ford 福特 Cadillac [ˈkædilæk] n. 卡迪拉克 Toyota 丰田 Mitsubishi 三菱 Subaru 斯巴鲁 Citroen 雪铁龙

wheel [wiːl]

核心词义	n. 轮子，车轮；方向盘；旋转	A wheel revolves round its axis. 轮子是绕轴旋转的。
拓展词义	v. 推，转动	He wheeled and faced his opponent squarely. 他转过身来面对着他的对手。
联想词汇	heel [hiːl] n. 脚后跟	

explosion [iksˈpləuʒən]

核心词义	n. 爆炸，爆发	The missile warhead hit the target, effecting a nuclear explosion. 导弹头命中目标，完成了一次核爆炸。
拓展词义	n. 激增，扩大	How can we account for the recent population explosion? 我们如何能解释最近人口激增的现象？

course [kɔːs]

核心词义	n. 跑道，路线，航线	The ship has altered its course. 这艘船改变了航线。
拓展词义	n. 课程，教程；过程，进程，行程；做法，一道菜（包含数盘菜）	The college course was then cut to three years. 大学学制那时缩短到三年。 There is an elaborate five-course meal. 这儿有五道菜的美餐。
习惯用法	of course 当然 in the course of 在……期间，在……过程中	

rival [ˈraivəl]

核心词义	n. 对手，竞争者	He beat his rival. 他击败了他的竞争对手。
拓展词义	v. 与……相匹敌，与……相竞争	None of us can rival him in strength. 我们谁也没他劲大。
词语辨析	rival 和 opponent 都有对手的含义。 rival 除了有对手的意思外，还有匹敌者的意思； opponent 有反对者的意思。	

speed [spiːd]

核心词义	v. (sped, sped) 加快，疾驶，飞跑	He sped his car through the street. 他开车飞速地穿过街道。
拓展词义	n. 速度，迅速	He drove at a speed of eighty miles an hour. 他以每小时 80 英里的速度开车。
习惯用法	at full speed 用全速，开足马力，尽力地 at speed 飞快地 speed up 加快速度	

downhill ['daunːhil]		
核心词义	*ad*. 下坡，向下	We picked up speed as we went downhill. 下山时我们的速度加快了。

Lesson

57

Can I help you, madam?
你要买什么，夫人？

madam ['mædəm]		
核心词义	n. 夫人，女士	Can I help you, madam? 女士，我能帮您什么忙吗?

jeans [dʒiːnz]		
核心词义	n. 牛仔裤	A woman in blue jeans walked into the store. 一个穿蓝色牛仔裤的妇女走进商店。

hesitate ['heziteit]		
核心词义	v. 犹豫，迟疑，踌躇	He hesitated before he answered because he didn't know what to say. 他在回答之前犹豫了一下，因为他不知道说什么。

serve [səːv]		
核心词义	v. 可作……用，服务，接待（顾客），供应	The manager of the restaurant has trained the waitress to serve correctly at table. 饭馆的经理训练过那位女服务员如何正确地招待顾客。 The restaurant serves nice food. 这家饭馆供应的饭菜不错。
联想词汇	deserve [di'zəːv] v. 应该得到	
习惯用法	serve as 充当，担任 serve in 在……就职	

scornfully [ˈskɔːnfuli]		
核心词义	ad. 轻蔑地	He scornfully talked about material things. 他轻蔑地谈起物质方面的享受。

punish [ˈpʌniʃ]		
核心词义	v. 惩罚，处罚	Motorists should be punished severely for dangerous driving. 汽车司机如危险驾驶应受到严厉处罚。

fur [fəː]		
核心词义	n. 裘皮；毛皮；软毛	She was wearing a silver fox fur across her shoulders. 她肩上披着一张银狐皮。

eager [ˈiːgə]		
核心词义	a. 渴望的，热切的	She listened with eager attention. 她聚精会神地倾听。
习惯用法	be eager for 渴望，渴求 be eager to do 渴望做某事	
联想词汇	keen [kiːn] a. 锋利的，敏锐的，强烈的，热切的	
词语辨析	eager，keen 都含渴望的意思。 eager 指以很大的热情渴望实现愿望或达到目的，有时也指由于其他感情影响而表现急不可耐的； keen 指对某人、某物怀有极大兴趣或热情的。	

Lesson

58

A blessing in disguise?
是因祸得福吗?

blessing ['blesiŋ]		
核心词义	n. 福分，服气	Sending you my blessing again. 再次寄上我的祝福。

disguise [dis'gaiz]		
核心词义	n. 假面目，假装	The spy's disguise was soon penetrated. 间谍的伪装不久便被识破了。
拓展词义	v. 假装，伪装，遮盖	It is impossible to disguise the fact that business is bad. 生意不好这件事无法隐瞒。
联想词汇	disgust [dis'gʌst] n. 厌恶，嫌恶 v. 令人厌恶	

tiny ['taini]		
核心词义	a. 极小的，微小的	The baby put his tiny hand in mine. 那个婴儿把小手放在我的手中。
词语辨析	small，little，tiny 都含小的意思。 small 指容量、面积、数量、体积等小的; little 指具体人或物小时，常有赞赏、爱怜等感情色彩; tiny 指极小的。	

possess [pə'zes]		
核心词义	v. 拥有，占有，支配	To possess wealth is not always to be happy. 拥有财富并非一定快乐。
习惯用法	be possessed of 拥有，占有，具有，享有 possess oneself of 取得，获得，把……占为己有	

cursed [ˈkɜːsid]

核心词义	a. 该诅咒的；可恨的	I wish that cursed dog would be quiet. 我希望那只讨厌的狗会安静下来。

plant [plɑːnt]

核心词义	v. 种植	Farmers plant seeds. 农民们播种。
拓展词义	n. 植物；工厂	Hot climate and plentiful rainfall favour the growth of plants. 炎热的气候和充足的雨水有助于植物生长。
联想词汇	plan [plæn] n. 计划，策略，方法 v. 计划，打算，设计 plantation [plæn'teiʃən] n. 种植园 transplant [træns'plɑːnt] vt. 移植（器官、皮肤、头发等）；（人）移居 　　　　　　　　　　　　n. （器官、皮肤、头发等）的移植	

church [tʃɜːtʃ]

核心词义	n. 教堂	There are three churches in this town. 这座城里有三个教堂。
拓展词义	n. 礼拜	Church begins at nine o'clock. 礼拜仪式九点开始。

evil [ˈiːvl]

核心词义	a. 邪恶的，坏的	He is an evil man with evil ideas, and leads an evil life. 他是一个满脑子邪恶念头的邪恶的人，过着一种罪恶的生活。
拓展词义	n. 邪恶，祸害	Love of money is the root of all evil. 爱钱是邪恶的根源。
联想词汇	devil [ˈdevl] n. 魔鬼，恶魔	

reputation [ˌrepju(ː)'teiʃən]

核心词义	n. 名誉，名声	This store has an excellent reputation for fair dealing. 该商店因买卖公道而享有极高的声誉。

claim [kleim]

核心词义	v. 要求，请求，主张，声称，说明，以……为其后果	He claimed that he hadn't done it, but I didn't believe him. 他声称没有做这件事，可是我不相信他。
拓展词义	n. 要求	His claim to own the house is valid. 他主张对此屋的所有权有效。
习惯用法	make a claim for 对（赔偿等）提出要求…… make a claim to 认为……是属于自己的	

victim ['viktim]

核心词义	n. 受害者	Most of the victims were shot in the back while trying to run away. 大多数受害者在设法逃跑时从背后被枪杀。

vicar ['vikə]

核心词义	n. 教区牧师	We were married by our local vicar. 我们是由本地教区牧师主持婚礼的。

source [sɔːs]

核心词义	n. 来源，源头；出处，原因	The news comes from a reliable source. 这条消息来源可靠。 This faulty connection is the source of the engine trouble. 这种错误的连接法是引擎出毛病的原因。
联想词汇	resource [ri'sɔːs] n. 资源，财力	

income [ˈinkʌm]		
核心词义	*n*. 收入,所得	He deceived his friends about his income. 他在自己的收入问题上欺骗了朋友。
词根词缀	in-向内 + come 来。该词为"向内进入的东西",即"收入"	

trunk [trʌŋk]		
核心词义	*n*. 树干	He cut off the branches from the trunk. 他把树干上的小分枝都剪掉。

Lesson

59

In or out?
进来还是出去？

bark [bɑːk]		
核心词义	*v.* 狗叫	The dog barks at strangers. 这只狗对陌生人吠叫。

press [pres]		
核心词义	*v.* 按，压	Press the button, then the machine will work. 按下电钮，机器就能转动了。
拓展词义	*n.* 新闻界； 按，压	The press is interested in sports. 新闻界对体育运动感兴趣。
习惯用法	press for 催逼；迫切要求 the press 新闻界，报界	

联想词汇	compress [kəm'pres] *v.* 压缩，压榨
	depress [di'pres] *v.* 使……沮丧
	express [iks'pres] *n.* 快车，快递，专使
	             a. 急速的，明确的
	             v. 表达，表示	

paw [pɔː]		
核心词义	*n.* 脚爪，爪子	This is a black cat with white paws. 这是一只长着白爪子的小黑猫。
联想词汇	claw [klɔː] *n.* 爪	

latch [lætʃ]		
核心词义	*n.* 门闩	To open the gate, lift up the latch. 要打开大门，先把门闩提起来。

expert ['ekspəːt]

核心词义	n . 专家，能手	The cook was an expert at making sauces. 那位厨师是调制味汁的能手。
拓展词义	a . 熟练的，内行的	To her expert eye, the painting was terrible. 以她内行的眼光看，这幅画槽透了。
习惯用法	be expert in/at... 在……方面是专家	

develop [di'veləp]

核心词义	v . 发展，开发	Fresh air and exercise develop healthy bodies. 新鲜空气和运动能使身体健康。
拓展词义	v . 冲洗照片；使成长，使发育；习惯	Can you develop this film for us? 你能代我们冲洗这个胶卷吗？
联想词汇	envelope ['enviləup] n . 信封	

habit ['hæbit]

核心词义	n . 习惯，脾性	My colleague has broken off the habit of smoking. 我的同事已经戒掉了吸烟的习惯。
习惯用法	get into the habit of 养成（染上）某习惯	
联想词汇	inhabit [in'hæbit] vt . 居住于，栖息于 prohibit [prə'hibit] vt . 禁止，阻止	

remove [ri'muːv]

核心词义	v . 移走，拆掉，取下；开除，移居	He removed the picture and put it in the drawer. 他把画取下来，放到抽屉里。 Our office has removed. 我们的机关迁移了。
习惯用法	be removed from 与……远离；与……疏远的	

The future
卜算未来

future [ˈfjuːtʃə]		
核心词义	*n*. 将来，未来，前途	The future lies before us. 未来展现在我们面前。
拓展词义	*a*. 未来的	She introduced him as her future husband. 她介绍说他是她的未婚夫。
习惯用法	in future 今后，往后 in the future 将来，未来	

fair [fɛə]		
核心词义	*n*. 展览会，市集	We participated in the spring fair. 我们参加了春季展览会。
拓展词义	*a*. 公平的，合理的；晴朗的	The umpire's duty is to see that competition is fair play. 裁判员的职责是监督双方进行公平竞争。 We met on a fair day. 我们在一个晴朗的日子见面了。

fortune-teller [ˈfɔːtʃən-ˌtelə]		
核心词义	*n*. 算命人	I went to the fortune-teller yesterday. 我昨天去算命了。

crystal [ˈkristl]		
核心词义	*n*. 水晶 *a*. 水晶般的，清澈的，清楚的	Those fine wine glasses are made of crystal. 那些漂亮的酒杯是用水晶做的。 It is crystal clear what we must do. 我们该做什么是很明显的。

relation [ri'leiʃən]		
核心词义	*n.* 关系，家人，亲戚	There's no relation between the two things. 这两件事没有联系。
联想词汇	relationship [ri'leiʃənʃip] *n.* 关系，关联 related [ri'leitid] *a.* 有关系的，有关联的	

impatiently [im'peiʃəntli]		
核心词义	*ad.* 不耐烦地	She waved them away impatiently. 她不耐烦地挥手让他们走开。
联想词汇	impatient [im'peiʃənt] *a.* 不耐烦的，急躁的	

Lesson

61

Trouble with the Hubble
哈勃望远镜的困难

telescope ['teliskəup]		
核心词义	n. 望远镜	She resolved to make a telescope. 她决心做一架望远镜。
联想词汇	scope [skəup] n. 范围，范畴，领域 microscope ['maikrəskəup] n. 显微镜	

launch [lɔːntʃ, lɑːntʃ]		
核心词义	v. 使下水；发动，发出，发射	He launched into a new subject last year. 他去年开始了一个新的课题。
拓展词义	n. 发射；汽艇，船下水	I saw the launch of the rocket yesterday. 我昨天看了火箭发射。
习惯用法	launch into 使在（水）中漂浮；发射上天；开始从事	

space [speis]		
核心词义	n. 空间	Keep some space between you and the car ahead. 跟前面的汽车保持一定距离。

billion ['biljən]		
核心词义	n. 十亿	The bank has assets of more than ￡1 billion. 该银行有 10 亿多英镑的资产。

faulty ['fɔːlti]		
核心词义	a. 有错误的，有缺点的	We traced the trouble to a faulty transformer. 我们查出故障出在一个有毛病的变压器上。

astronaut [ˈæstrənɔːt]		
核心词义	n. 宇航员	There're three astronauts in the spacecraft. 在这艘宇宙飞船里有三名宇航员。
联想词汇	astrogation [ˌæstrəˈgeiʃən] n. 宇宙航行学	
词根词缀	词缀-astro 表示"宇宙，天体"的含义	

shuttle [ˈʃʌtl]		
核心词义	n. 航天飞机；（短程运行穿梭的飞机或火车、汽车）	The U. S. made the first space shuttle in the world. 美国制造了世界上第一架航天飞机。

Endeavour [inˈdevə(r)]		
核心词义	n. "奋进"号；努力，尽力	She made every endeavor to help us. 她尽力地去帮助我们。
拓展词义	v. 尝试，试图	He endeavored after more fame and wealth. 他力图获得更大的名声和更多的财富。

robot arm [ˈrəubɔt-ˌɑːm]		
核心词义	n. 机器手	A robot arm can work intelligently. 机械手可以智能地工作。

grab [græb]		
核心词义	v. 抓取，抢去	Joe grabbed him by the collar. 乔抓住他的衣领。
拓展词义	n. 抓握，接应，掠夺	The thief made a grab at my bag but I pushed him away. 贼想抢我的手提包，但被我推开了。
习惯用法	grab hold of 抓紧	

atmosphere [ˈætməsfiə]		
核心词义	n. 大气，大气层	Changes in the climate are due to pollution of the atmosphere. 由于对大气层的污染而造成了气候变化。

拓展词义	*n*. 气氛，环境	There is an atmosphere of peace and calm in the country quite different from the atmosphere of a big city. 在乡间有一种和平宁静的气氛，与大城市的气氛截然不同。
联想词汇	sphere［sfiə］*a*. 球体的 *n*. 范围，领域，球，球体	

distant［'distənt］

核心词义	*a*. 遥远的，远的	That is a distant country. 那是一个遥远的国度。

universe［'juːnivəːs］

核心词义	*n*. 宇宙；星系，银河系	Our world is but a small part of the universe. 我们的地球只是宇宙的一小部分。
联想词汇	university［ˌjuːni'vəːsiti］*n*. 大学 universal［ˌjuːni'vəːsəl］*a*. 普遍的，通用的，宇宙的	

galaxy［'gæləksi］

核心词义	*n*. 银河；一群显赫之人	The earth is one of the planets in the Galaxy. 地球是银河系中的星球之一。 The company has a galaxy of talent. 该公司拥有一批优秀的人才。

eagle eye［'iːgl-'ai］

核心词义	*n*. 鹰眼；锐利的眼神	His father's eagle eye is always on him. 他父亲的锐利目光总是盯着他。

Lesson

62

After the fire
大火之后

control [kən'trəul]		
核心词义	*v.*/*n.* 克制，控制，支配，管理	A captain controls his ship and its crew. 船长管理他的船和船上的船员。 She explained the controls of the washing machine. 她解释了这台洗衣机的控制系统。
习惯用法	out of control 失去控制	
联想词汇	enroll [in'rəul] *v.* 登记，使加入 roller ['rəulə] *n.* 滚筒，滚轴，滚转机 roll [rəul] *n.* 卷，滚动，名单 　　　　　 *v.* 使打滚，转动；左右摇晃	

smoke [sməuk]		
核心词义	*v.* 吸烟 *n.* 烟	The house is full of smoke. 满屋子都是烟。 The doctor told me not to smoke. 医生告诫我不要抽烟。
联想词汇	smoking ['sməukiŋ] *n.* 吸烟 smoker ['sməukə] *n.* 吸烟者	

desolate ['desəlit]		
核心词义	*a.* 荒凉的；凄凉的	The house was desolate, ready to be torn down. 这房子没人居住，等着拆除。

拓展词义	*v.* 毁坏，使沮丧	War has desolated that city. 战争毁坏了那座城市。

threaten [ˈθretn]

核心词义	*v.* 恐吓，威胁；预示（某事）	Don't try to threaten me. I won't compromise with you. 不要威胁我，我不会和你妥协的。

surrounding [səˈraundiŋ]

核心词义	*a.* 周围的	The surrounding villages have been absorbed by/into the growing city. 周围的村庄已经并入了那不断扩展的城市。
联想词汇	surround [səˈraund] *vt.* 包围，环绕 around [əˈraund] *ad.* 大约，到处，在周围 　　　　　　　*prep.* 在……周围 round [raund] *n.* 圆，范围，巡回 　　　　　　*a.* 圆的，完全的 　　　　　　*v.* 使成圆形，绕行 　　　　　　*prep.* 在……四周，位于……；遍及，围绕 　　　　　　*ad.* 到处，各处，大约，大概	

destruction [disˈtrʌkʃən]

核心词义	*n.* 破坏，毁灭	The enemy bombs caused widespread destruction. 敌人的炸弹造成大面积的破坏。
词根词缀	de- 相反 + struct 建造 + -ion 名词后缀	

flood [flʌd]

核心词义	*n.* 洪水，水灾	The floods were a cataclysm from which the local people never recovered. 经历了这场特大洪水，当地人民元气大伤，很难恢复。

拓展词义	v. 大量涌来，充满，泛滥	Our street floods whenever we have rain. 我们的街道一下雨就淹水。 Letters flooded the office. 办公室里到处是信件。

authority [ɔː'θɔriti]

核心词义	n. 权力，权威，当局	A good dictionary is an authority on the meanings of words. 一本好词典是词义的权威。 The local authorities decided to build a suspension bridge over the river. 该地区政府决定在这条河上建一座吊桥。
联想词汇	author ['ɔːθə] n. 作者 auxiliary [ɔːg'ziljəri] a. 附加的，辅助的	

grass-seed [grɑːs-ˌsiːd]

核心词义	n. 草籽	They planted grass-seed on the desolate hills. 他们在那些荒凉的山丘上撒播草籽。

spray [sprei]

核心词义	v. 喷	Water sprayed out all over me. 水喷出来浇了我一身。
拓展词义	n. 浪花，飞沫；喷雾	We were wet with the sea spray. 我们被海水的浪花溅湿。
联想词汇	ray [rei] n. 光线，射线	

quantity ['kwɔntiti]

核心词义	n. 量，数量，大量	Mathematics is the science of pure quantity. 数学是研究纯数量的科学。

root [ru:t]

核心词义	n. 根，根源	The roots of this plant go deep. 这种植物的根扎得很深。 Money is the root of all evil. 金钱是万恶之源。

century ['sentʃuri,-tʃəri]

核心词义	n. 世纪	The 5th century saw the end of the Roman Empire in the West. 古罗马帝国灭亡于5世纪。

patch [pætʃ]

核心词义	n. 小片，补丁	He had a patch on the elbow of his jacket. 他的上衣肘部有一块补丁。
拓展词义	v. 补，修理，调停	Give me some cloth to patch your trousers. 给我一点儿布来补你的裤子。 The workman patched the ceiling. 工人修补了天花板。
联想词汇	dispatch [dis'pætʃ] v. 派遣，调遣，匆匆吃完 n. 派遣，急件	
词语辨析	mend，repair，patch 含修理、修补的意思。 mend 系常用词，指修补破损的简单日常用具，使之可再用； repair 指修理构造较复杂或损坏较严重的物体，使之再次完整； patch 指补缀、填补，使之可再用。	

blacken ['blækən]

核心词义	v. 使……黑，变黑，发暗	His face was blackened with coal. 他的脸被煤弄黑了。
词根词缀	black 黑 + -en 使变成	

Lesson

63

She was not amused
她并不觉得好笑

---

circle [ˈsəːkl]

核心词义	*n*. 圆周，圈子，社交圈，周期	There is a circle of flowers around the statue. 塑像周围鲜花围绕。
拓展词义	*v*. 包围，盘旋，环绕	They saw the birds were circling again. 他们看见鸟儿又在盘旋。
联想词汇	circumstance [ˈsəːkəmstəns] *n*. 环境，状况，事件 circular [ˈsəːkjulə] *a*. 循环的，圆形的 *n*. 传单，通报 circumference [səˈkʌmfərəns] *n*. 圆周，周围	

---

admire [ədˈmaiə]

核心词义	*v*. 钦佩，羡慕，赞美	We admire at your fortune. 我们羡慕你的好运气。
习惯用法	admire at 对……感到羡慕（惊讶） admire 因……而称赞	

---

close [kləuz]

核心词义	*a*. 靠近的，亲密的；浓缩的，势均力敌的	I live close to the shops. 我住得离商店很近。
拓展词义	*v*. 关闭，终止 *n*. 终结，结束	At eleven the meeting closed. 会议于11点结束。
联想词汇	enclose [inˈkləuz] *vt*. 围绕，圈起，封入 closet [ˈkləzit] *n*. 壁橱，小室 enclosure [inˈkləuʒə] *n*. 围住，圈住，封入，附件	

习惯用法	close with 靠近，逼近，接受 close down（工厂等的）关闭，停歇；封闭

wedding ['wediŋ]

核心词义	n. 婚礼	She wants them to sing at her wedding. 她要他们在她的婚礼上唱歌。
联想词汇	diamond wedding 钻石婚礼（结婚 60 周年或 75 周年纪念） golden wedding 金婚（结婚 50 周年纪念） silver wedding 银婚（结婚 25 周年纪念） tin wedding 锡婚（结婚 10 周年纪念） wooden wedding 木婚（结婚 5 周年纪念）		

reception [ri'sepʃən]

核心词义	n. 接待，欢迎，接受	Their school gave a reception to their new principal. 他们学校为新校长举办了一个招待会。
联想词汇	receptionist [ri'sepʃənist] n. 接待员 perception [pə'sepʃən] n. 感觉，知觉 receipt [ri'si:t] n. 收据	

sort [sɔːt]

核心词义	n. 种类，类别；某一种人，某一类人	I was sort of hoping to leave early today. 我今天有点儿想早点走。
拓展词义	v. 分类，整理	The salesman sorted his new consignment of stockings. 推销员把新到的一批长袜清理分类。
习惯用法	sort of 有几分，有那么点儿 sort out 整理；弄清楚	

Lesson

64

The channel Tunnel
海峡隧道

---

tunnel ['tʌnl]

核心词义	n. 隧道，地下道	The train passed through a tunnel. 火车通过了一条隧道。

port ['pɔːt]

核心词义	n. 港口	This is an excellent port being secure from every wind. 这个海港是一个不论刮什么样的风都不会出危险的良港。

ventilate ['ventileit]

核心词义	v. 使……空气流通，给……装通风设备	We ventilate a room by opening windows. 我们开窗以使室内空气流通。

chimney ['tʃimni]

核心词义	n. 烟囱	The factory chimneys poured smoke into the air. 工厂的烟囱向空中排烟。

sea level ['siː-lev(ə)l]

核心词义	海平面	This mountain is 1,400 meters above sea level. 这座山海拔 1400 米。

double ['dʌbl]

核心词义	a. 两倍的，双的	The total output is double that of last year. 总产量是去年的两倍。

拓展词义	n. 两倍 v. 把……对折，使加倍	Ten is the double of five. 10 是 5 的两倍。 She doubled the sheet of the paper and put it away. 她把这张纸折起来放到一边。
联想词汇	doubt [daut] n. 怀疑，疑惑 v. 怀疑，不信	

ventilation [venti'leiʃən]

核心词义	n. 通风；空气流通	The office has recently been refurbished and the ventilation system improved. 这间办公室最近重新修缮油漆过，通风系统得到了改善。

fear [fiə]

核心词义	v. 害怕，恐惧，担心	Never fear — I will hold your hand. 别怕，我会握住你的手。
拓展词义	n. 恐惧，害怕	There's not much fear of frost at this time of year. 每年这个时候，就不用担心会下霜冻了。
习惯用法	be in fear (of)（为……而）提心吊胆	

invasion [in'veiʒən]

核心词义	n. 侵入，侵略	The invasion of tourists brought life to the summer resort. 大批游客涌入，使这个避暑胜地热闹起来。

officially [ə'fiʃəli]

核心词义	ad. 官方地，正式地	This new library was officially opened last week. 这家新图书馆上星期正式起用。

connect [kə'nekt]

核心词义	v. 连接	We connect the word "blue" with the color of the sky. 我们由"蓝"这个字会联想到晴空的颜色。

习惯用法	connect with 和……有联系，和……有关 connect to 连接；结合
词语辨析	join，combine，connect 含联合、结合、接合的意思。 join 指任何事物的直接连接，连接的程度可紧可松，还能分开之意； combine 着重指两个或两个以上的人或事物为了共同目的而结合在一起，结合后原来部分可能仍不改变或失去其本性； connect 指通过某种媒介物把事物连接起来，原物的特征还保持。

European [ˌjuərəˈpi(ː)ən]

核心词义	a. 欧洲的 n. 欧洲人	She is the only European in the class. 她是班上唯一的欧洲人。

continent [ˈkɔntinənt]

核心词义	n. 大陆，洲	Africa is a continent，but Greenland is not. 非洲是大陆，而格陵兰不是。

Lesson

65

Jumbo versus the police
小象对警察

versus [ˈvɜːsəs]		
核心词义	*prep.* 对（略作 V. 或 vs.）	The most exciting game was Harvard versus Yale. 最富紧张刺激的球赛是哈佛队对耶鲁队。

Christmas [ˈkrisməs]		
核心词义	*n.* 圣诞节	I wish you a merry Christmas. 祝你圣诞快乐。

circus [ˈsɜːkəs]		
核心词义	*n.* 马戏团	The circus is coming here next week. 马戏团下星期来这儿。

present [ˈpreznt]		
核心词义	*n.* 礼物；现在	He gave me a handsome present. 他给我一份很好的礼物。
拓展词义	*a.* 现在的，出席的，当面的 *v.* 赠送，提出，呈现	We presented him a basketball on his birthday. 他生日那天我们送给他一个篮球。 How many people were present at the meeting? 会议有多少人出席？
习惯用法	at present 现在，目前 for the present 暂时，暂且 present oneself 出席，到场	

联想词汇	presence ['prezəns] n. 出席，在场 absence ['æbsəns] n. 缺乏，缺少，缺席 represent [ˌrepri'zent] vt. 表现，表示，描绘，代表

accompany [ə'kʌmpəni]

核心词义	v. 陪伴，随行； 为……伴奏	She accompanied me to the doctor's. 她陪我去看的医生。
习惯用法	(be) accompanied by 附有，伴随 be-accompanied with (a thing) 带着，带有，兼有	
联想词汇	companion [kəm'pænjən] n. 同伴，同事	

approach [ə'prəutʃ]

核心词义	v. 靠近，接近； 接洽，动手 处理	He approached the new job with enthusiasm. 他满怀热情地去做新的工作。 He approached the question as a scientist. 他以一个科学家的眼光去处理这个问题。
习惯用法	at the approach of 在……快到的时候 make approach to sb. 设法接近某人 approach to 接近，近似 approach sb. on/about sth. 向某人接洽、商量	
联想词汇	reproach [ri'prəutʃ] n./v. 责备，耻辱 appropriate [ə'prəupri:ət] a. 适当的 approximate [ə'prɔksimeit] a. 大约的，近似的	

ought [ɔːt]

核心词义	v. aux. 应该， 应当	It ought to be a fine day tomorrow morning. 明天早晨天气应该不错。

weigh [wei]

核心词义	v. 秤重量；权衡	We should weigh the advantages and disadvantages on this matter. 我们在这件事情上需要权衡一下利弊。

联想词汇	weight [weit] *n*. 重量，体重，重担

fortunate ['fɔːtʃənit]

核心词义	*a*. 幸运的，侥幸的	The lack of good diagnostic test isn't fortunate. 缺乏好的诊断性测试是不利的。

Lesson

66

Sweet as honey!
像蜜一样甜！

bomber [ˈbɔmə]		
核心词义	*n.* 轰炸机	He flew a bomber during the war. 他在战时驾驶轰炸机。

remote [riˈməut]		
核心词义	*a.* 偏僻的，遥远的	At night I like to look at the remote stars in the clear sky. 晚上我喜欢观看晴朗的夜空中遥远的星星。
拓展词义	*a.* （亲戚上的）远的；疏远的	The thing happened in the remote past. 这件事发生在遥远的过去。 Her manner was polite but remote. 她彬彬有礼，却十分冷淡。
联想词汇	promote [prəˈməut] *vt.* 促进，提升，策划	

Pacific [pəˈsifik]		
核心词义	*n.* 太平洋	These creatures live in the depth of the Pacific Ocean. 这些生物生活在太平洋的海底。

damage [ˈdæmidʒ]		
核心词义	*v.* 破坏，毁坏	The flood did a lot of damage to the crops. 洪水毁坏了大量农作物。

wreck [rek]		
核心词义	*n.* 失事船（或飞机），残骸，（船，飞机的）失事	The shores are strewn with wrecks. 海岸上布满失事船只的残骸。

rediscover [ˈriːdisˈkʌvə]

核心词义	v . 重新发现	Your love has helped me to rediscover myself. 你的爱让我重新发现我自己。

aerial [ˈɛəriəl]

核心词义	a . 空中的，航空的	Aerial pollution is a problem that should be solved quickly. 空气污染是一个亟待解决的问题。

survey [səˈvei]

核心词义	n . 调查	The reporter is doing a survey of public attitudes. 那位记者正在进行民意调查。
拓展词义	v . 纵览，勘察，检查	I surveyed the view from the top of the hill. 我从山顶眺望景色。 Survey the car before you buy it. 买车之前先对它鉴定一下。

rescue [ˈreskjuː]

核心词义	v . 援救，救出，营救	They rescued the child. 他们救出了那个孩子。
拓展词义	n . 营救，援救	They are performing an attempt of a rescue. 他们正在进行营救行动。
习惯用法	rescue from 救出……	

package [ˈpækidʒ]

核心词义	v . 包装，把……打包	They package their goods in attractive wrappers. 他们把货物包在好看的包装袋里。
拓展词义	n . 包裹，包装	He brought me a large package. 他给我送来一个大包裹。

enthusiast [in'θju:ziæst]

核心词义	n. 热心人	He is a sport enthusiast. 他是一个体育爱好者。
联想词汇	enthusiasm [in'θju:ziæzəm] n. 热情，热心；热衷的事物	

restore [ris'tɔ:]

核心词义	v. 修复；使恢复；归还	The old painting was damaged in the flood and had to be painstakingly restored. 那幅古画在洪水中遭到毁坏，必须精心修复。
联想词汇	store [stɔ:, stəə] n. 商店，贮藏，仓库　　v. 贮藏，贮备，存储　storage ['stɔridʒ] n. 储存体，储藏，仓库	

imagine [i'mædʒi]

核心词义	v. 想象，幻想，猜测	I can imagine the scene clearly in my mind. 我可以清楚地想象出那个情景。There's nobody following us — you're just imagining it! 没有人跟着我们——你只不过是猜想而已。
联想词汇	image ['imidʒ] n. 图像，影像，肖像，想象	

packing case ['pækiŋ-keis]

核心词义	n. 包装箱	His new TV came in a big packing case. 他新购的电视机是装在一只大的包装箱内运来的。

colony ['kɔləni]

核心词义	n. （动植物的）群体，集群	There lived a colony of bees on the tree. 树上生活着一群蜜蜂。
拓展词义	n. 殖民地；聚居地	They amassed huge wealth by plundering the colonies. 他们通过掠夺殖民地聚敛了大笔的财富。

bee [biː]

核心词义	n. 蜂	The bee is going from flower to flower. 那只蜜蜂在花丛间飞来飞去。

hive [haiv]

核心词义	n. 蜂房，蜂箱	The hive is made of wood. 这蜂箱是用木材做的。
拓展词义	n. 蜂群	The whole hive was busy. 整个蜂群都在忙碌。

preserve [priˈzəːv]

核心词义	v. 保护，保持，维持	It's the duty of the police to preserve the public order. 维护公共秩序是警察的职责。

beeswax [ˈbiːzwæks]

核心词义	n. 蜂蜡	A colony of bees had turned the engine into a hive and it was totally preserved in beeswax! 一群蜜蜂把发动机当作了蜂房，发动机在蜂蜡中被完整地保存了下来。

Lesson

67

Volcanoes
火山

---

volcano [vɔlˈkeinəu]

核心词义	*n*. 火山	The eruption of a volcano is spontaneous. 火山的爆发是自发的。

active [ˈæktiv]

核心词义	*a*. 积极的，主动的	She is an active girl. 她是一位活泼的姑娘。 He is an active member of the club. 他是俱乐部的积极分子。

Congo [ˈkɔŋgəu]

核心词义	*n*. 刚果	What's the area of the Congo in square miles? 刚果的面积是多少平方英里？

erupt [iˈrʌpt]

核心词义	*v*. 爆发，突然发生	Laughter erupted from the audience. 笑声从观众席上爆发出来。

violently [ˈvaiələntli]

核心词义	*a*. 猛烈的，激烈的，极端的	I felt my heart beat violently. 我感觉到自己的心跳得很厉害。

manage [ˈmænidʒ]

核心词义	*v*. 处理，管理，控制	He managed the supermarket when the owner was away. 当店主不在的时候，他管理这个超级市场。

brilliant [ˈnriljənt]

核心词义	*a*. 精彩的；灿烂的，杰出的	The moon was brilliant. 月光明亮极了。 He came up with a brilliant idea. 他想出了一个绝妙的主意。

liquid [ˈlikwid]

核心词义	*a*. 液体的，液态的，流动的 *n*. 液体	Water is both a fluid and a liquid. 水既是流体又是液体。

escape [isˈkeip]

核心词义	*v*. 逃脱，避开，溜走	None of them could escape. 他们谁也跑不了。
拓展词义	*n*. 逃走，逃脱	We quickly cut off the enemy's escape. 我们迅速切断了敌人的退路。
习惯用法	escape from 从……漏出；从……逃脱	

alive [əˈlaiv]

核心词义	*a*. 活着的；有活力的，有生气的	He is the happinest man alive. 他是世界上最快乐的人。
习惯用法	alive with 充满……	
联想词汇	live [laiv] *a*. 活的，生动的，精力充沛的，直播的 　　　　　*v*. 活，生存；居住 lively [ˈlaivli] *a*. 活泼的，醒目的，剧烈的 living [ˈliviŋ] *a*. 活着的，在使用中，生动的 　　　　　*n*. 生计，生活方式	
词汇辨析	living, alive, live 都含活的意思。 living 用于生物时，指活着的； alive 指活着的、在世的，着重于状态，它用作表语，或放有名词或代词后作定语； live 只用于物，指活的。	

Lesson

68

Persistent
纠缠不休

persistent [pə'sistənt]		
核心词义	*a*. 坚持的，固执的	Albert had a persistent headache that lasted for three days. 艾伯特连续头痛了三天。
词根词缀	词根-sist 表示"坚持，承受"的含义。例如：consist [kən'sist] *vt*. 组成，存在，一致	
联想词汇	exist [ig'zist] *v*. 存在 assist [ə'sist] *v*. 协助 *n*. 帮助，协助 resist [ri'zist] *v*. 抵抗，耐得住，压制 consistent [kən'sistənt] *a*. 始终如一的，一致的，坚持的	
词语辨析	continue，last，persist 含继续、延续的意思。 continue 指持续而无终止，通常强调不间断； last 指持久、延续； persist 指持续存在下去。	

avoid [ə'vɔid]		
核心词义	*v*. 避免，避开	To avoid confusion, the teams wore different colors. 为避免混淆，两队分穿不同颜色的衣服。
联想词汇	void [vɔid] *a*. 空的	
词语辨析	escape，evade，avoid 含避免、逃避的意思。 escape 指脱离或避开即将来临或近在眼前的伤害、危险、灾祸等事物常作借喻用； evade 强调用心机或狡猾的手段逃避或回避对自己不利的东西； avoid 强调有意识地躲避不愉快的或可能发生危险的事物或情况。	

insist [in'sist]		
核心词义	*v.* 坚持；坚决宣称，坚持要求	You must insist on everything being done on the square. 你们必须坚持开诚布公地办一切事情。
习惯用法	insist on 坚持；坚决主张 insist that 主张；坚持	

Lesson 69

But not murder!
并非谋杀！

murder ['məːdə]		
核心词义	v./n. 谋杀	He was charged with murder but they found him innocent of the charge. 他被控告谋杀，但人们发现他是无辜的。

instruct [in'strʌkt]		
核心词义	v. 教，命令；指导，传授	The union issued an order instructing its members not to work overtime. 工会发出指示，不让会员超时工作。 She instructs music once a week at a middle school. 她在中学每周教一次音乐课。
联想词汇	construct [kən'strʌkt] vt. 构造，建造，想出 destruct [dis'trʌkt] vt. 破坏	

acquire [ə'kwaiə]		
核心词义	v. 获得，取得，学到	The company has recently acquired new offices in central London. 公司最近在伦敦市中心弄到了新的办公室。
词语辨析	get，obtain，acquire，gain 都含得到、获得的意思。 get 指以某种方法或手段得到某种东西； obtain 是较正式用语，常指通过努力工作请求而得到所需的东西；	

acquire 强调经过漫长的努力过程而逐渐获得；
gain 往往指通过努力或有意识行动而获得某种有益或有利的东西。

confidence [ˈkɔnfidəns]		
核心词义	*n.* 信任，信心	Confidence is half of victory. 自信就是成功的一半。

examiner [igˈzæminə]		
核心词义	*n.* 主考官	I submitted my papers to the examiner. 我把试卷交给主考老师。
词根词缀	examine 考试 + -er 人	

suppose [səˈpəuz]		
核心词义	*v.* 推想，假设，以为，认为	I should suppose him to be about twenty. 我猜他是 20 岁左右。
拓展词义	*conj.* 如果	Suppose he can't come, who will do the work? 如果他不能前来，谁来做这项工作呢？
习惯用法	be supposed to (do) 本应该…… suppose that 假定 suppose + 名词/代词 + 动词不定式 猜想某人做某事	
词根词缀	sup- = sub- 在……下面 + pose 放着	

tap [tæp]		
核心词义	*v.* 轻打，轻敲	This music sets your feet tapping. 这音乐能使你的双脚不由自主地跟着打拍子。
拓展词义	*n.* 塞子，龙头；轻拍	Connect the hose to the tap and turn on the water. 把软管接在龙头上，打开水龙头。
联想词汇	pat [pæt] *n. / v.* 轻拍	

react [riˈækt]

核心词义	v. 反应，起作用，对抗	The audience reacted readily to his speech. 观众对他的演讲立即起了反应。
习惯用法	react against 反抗，反对 react to 对……做出反应 react on/upon 对……起作用，对……有影响	

brake [breik]

核心词义	n. 闸，刹车	His brakes failed on a steep hill. 他的刹车在陡峭的山路上失灵了。
拓展词义	v. 刹车	She braked suddenly to avoid the dog. 为了不撞着那条狗，她紧急刹车。
联想词汇	break [breik] n. 休息，中断，破裂 　　　　　　 v. 打破，弄破，弄坏 　　　　　　 vt. 违反，终止，透露，打破（纪录） bake [beik] v. 烘焙，烤	

pedal [ˈpedl]

核心词义	n. 踏板	He pressed down the accelerator pedal of his car. 他踩下汽车的加速器踏板。

mournful [ˈmɔːnful]

核心词义	a. 哀痛的，悲哀的，令人惋惜的	She sighed and looked mournful. 她叹了口气，显得很伤心。

Lesson

70

Red for danger
危险的红色

---

bullfight [ˈbulfait]

核心词义	n. 斗牛	Have you ever seen a bullfight in Spain? 你看过西班牙斗牛吗?

drunk [drʌŋk]

核心词义	n. 醉汉 a. 喝醉了的	There were a lot of drunk drivers on the roads on Saturday nights. 星期六的晚上马路上有很多酒后驾车者。

ring [riŋ]

核心词义	n. 圆形竞技场地	There is a clown who is showing in the middle of the ring. 有个小丑在剧场的中间表演。

unaware [ˌʌnəˈwɛə]

核心词义	a. 没察觉的	They were unaware that war was near. 他们不知道战争即将爆发。
联想词汇	aware [əˈwɛə] a. 知道的,意识到的 ware [wɛə] n. 制品,器具,货物	
词语辨析	aware,conscious,sensible 含有意识到的意思。 aware 侧重感官所意识到的外界事物; conscious 侧重心理感知; sensible 指可用感官察觉到的较复杂或抽象的事物的。	

bull [bul]

核心词义	n. 公牛	This is a bull. 这是一头公牛。

matador ['mætədɔː]

核心词义	n. 斗牛士	The bull was busy with the matador at the time. 当时那公牛正忙于对付斗牛士。

remark [ri'mɑːk]

核心词义	n. 评论，言语	His remark hurt her feelings. 他的话伤了她的感情。

apparently [ə'pærəntli]

核心词义	ad. 显然地	Apparently they're intending to put up the price of water. 看来他们要提高水费了。
词根词缀	appar = appear 出现、显露 + -ly 副词后缀	

sensitive ['sensitiv]

核心词义	a. 敏感的，灵敏的，易受伤害的	She is sensitive to what people think of her. 她很敏感人们对她是怎么想的。
习惯用法	be sensitive to 对……敏感，易感受……	
联想词汇	sensation [sen'seiʃən] n. 感觉，知觉；激动，轰动 sensible ['sensəbl] a. 明理的，明智的 sentimental [ˌsenti'mentl] a. 伤感的，多愁善感的，感情用事的	

criticism ['kritisiz(ə)m]

核心词义	n. 批评，评论	Some youth today do not allow any criticism at all. 现在有些年轻人根本指责不得。

charge [tʃɑːdʒ]

核心词义	v. 命令，告诫，加罪于，冲上去，收费，使充电	We charged and the enemy's front line fell back. 我们一冲锋，敌人的阵线就后退了。 He charged me to arrange everything. 他要我去安排一切事务。

拓展词义	*n.* 电荷，费用，掌管，指示	The old servant fulfilled his master's charge to care for the children. 老仆人履行了其主人要他照料孩子的指示。
习惯用法		at one's own charge（s）自费，用自己的钱 bring a charge of sth. against sb. 指控某人犯……罪 give sb. charge over 委托某人照管；授权某人管理 have（the）charge of 负责……，主管…… in charge 主管，负责，掌管，在……管辖之下，由……照顾 in the charge of sb. 由某人负责，由某人照料（管理） on a charge of 因……罪，因……嫌疑 charge oneself with 承担（工作），接受（任务） charge（up）to 把……记入（账册等），把……归咎于
联想词汇		discharge [dis'tʃɑːdʒ] *v.* 卸下，放出，解雇，放电，解除
词语辨析		charge, accuse 都含控告、谴责的意思。 charge 指因犯较大错误或重大罪行而进行正式法律控诉； accuse 指当面指控或指责，不一定诉诸法庭。

clumsily ['klʌmzili]

核心词义	*ad.* 笨拙地	Headcrabs move clumsily but quickly. 头蟹移动得很笨拙却很迅速。

bow [bau]

核心词义	*v.* 鞠躬，低头	The guilty man bowed his head in shame. 那个有罪的人羞愧地低下了头。

safety ['seifti]

核心词义	*n.* 平安，安全地带	The safety of the ship is the captain's responsibility. 确保船的安全是船长的责任。

sympathetically [ˌsimpə'θetikəli]

核心词义	*ad.* 同情地	He is looking at her sympathetically. 他同情地望着他。

Lesson

71

A famous clock
一个著名的大钟

parliament [ˈpɑːləmənt]		
核心词义	*n*. 议会，国会	The British Parliament consists of the House of Lords and the House of Commons. 英国议会由上院和下院组成。

erect [iˈrekt]		
核心词义	*v*. 竖立，使……直立	They erected a telephone pole. 他们竖起一根电话线杆子。
拓展词义	*a*. 直立的，竖立的，笔直的	There is an erect pine. 那儿有一棵挺拔的松树。
词语辨析	upright，erect 都含直立的意思。upright 指垂直的或直立而不倾斜的；erect 指（身体或物件）挺直而不弯曲的，其直立程度弱于 upright。	

accurate [ˈækjurit]		
核心词义	*a*. 准确的，精确的	He has made an accurate measurement of my garden. 他准确地丈量了我的花园。
联想词汇	secure [siˈkjuə] *a*. 无虑的，安心的，安全的 *v*. 固定，使……安全 cure [kjuə] *n*./*v*. 治疗，治愈，治疗法	

official [ə'fiʃəl]

核心词义	n. 官员，行政人员	The President and the Secretary of State are government officials. 总统和国务卿是政府官员。
拓展词义	a. 官方的，正式的；公务的	They have got some official figures. 他们得到一些官方数字。

Greenwich ['greinitʃ]

核心词义	n. 格林尼治	A tribe of arlists live in Greenwich village. 在格林尼治村住着许多艺术家。

observatory [əb'zə:vətəri]

核心词义	n. 天文台，气象台，瞭望台	Guy's house was close to the observatory. 盖伊的房子离天文台很近。
联想词汇	observe [əb'zə:v] v. 观察，遵守，注意到 reserve [ri'zə:v] n. 预备品，贮存 v. 保留，预订	
词根词缀	observ [e] + -atory 表示地方，观测天象的地方	

check [tʃek]

核心词义	v. 检查，阻止，核对	The hotel insists that guests check out of their rooms before 12 o'clock in the morning. 这家旅馆一定要客人在上午12点钟前结账后离开房间。
拓展词义	n. 检查，支票	I found a check that bounced. 我发现一张被退回的支票。
习惯用法	check in 报到；登记 check on 检查，阻止 check out 结账后离开，办妥手续离去	

microphone [ˈmaikrəfəun]

核心词义	n. 麦克风，扩音器	The singer used a microphone so that every one in the hall could hear him. 歌手用了麦克风，以便大厅里的每一个人都能听得见。

tower [ˈtauə]

核心词义	n. 塔，高楼	The tower is fifty feet in height. 塔高 50 英尺。

A car called Bluebird
"蓝鸟" 汽车

72

racing ['reisiŋ]		
核心词义	*n.* 竞赛；赛马	I think my racing car is the fastest (one). 我想我的赛车是跑得最快的（一辆）了。
联想词汇	racial ['reiʃəl] *a.* 种族的	

per [pəː, pə]		
核心词义	*prep.* 每，每一；依照，根据	You bought goods per list price. 你按照所列价格买商品。 These apples cost 40 pence per pound. 这些苹果每磅 40 便士。
习惯用法	as per 按照	

horsepower ['hɔːsˌpauəl]		
核心词义	*n.* 马力	This engine puts out more than one thousand horsepower. 这台发动机可产生 1000 以上的马力。

burst [bəːst]		
核心词义	*v.* (burst, burst) 爆裂，突发，挤满，突然打开	The dam burst under the weight of water. 那水坝在水的压力下决口了。 The storm burst and we all got wet. 暴风雨突然袭来，我们都淋湿了。
拓展词义	*n.* 破裂，爆发	There was a burst of laughter in the next room. 隔壁房间里突然爆发出一阵笑声。

习惯用法	at a burst 一阵；一口气 burst into 闯入；突然出现 burst out 大呼；惊叫 burst through 冲开；冲破

average ['ævəridʒ]

核心词义	a. 一般的，通常的，平均的	The average age of the boys in this class is fifteen. 本班男生的平均年龄是 15 岁。
拓展词义	n. 平均，平均数 v. 求……的平均数	An average of 1,500 persons passes here every day. 每天平均有 1500 个人经过此地。 If you average 4, 5 and 9, you get 6. 如果你求 4, 5 和 9 的平均数，得 6。

footstep ['futstep]

核心词义	n. 脚步（声），足迹	He heard soft footsteps coming up the stair. 他听见有人上楼的轻微脚步声。
联想词汇	step [setp] n. 步骤，脚步，足迹	

Lesson
73
The record-holder
纪录保持者

record-holder [ˈrekɔːd-ˈhəuldə]		
核心词义	纪录保持者	He is the new record-holder of 100-metre-dash. 他是百米纪录的保持者。
联想词汇	holder [ˈhəuldə] n. 持有人，所有人，支持物 record [ˈrekɔːd] v. 记录，将（声音等）录下 n. 记录，最好的成绩	

truant [ˈtruːənt]		
核心词义	n. 逃学的孩子	The teacher told me that there were 2 traunts in her class. 这个老师告诉我她班有 2 个逃课生。

unimaginative [ˌʌniˈmædʒinətiv]		
核心词义	a. 缺乏想象力的	Adults are more unimaginative than children. 成年人会比小孩子更缺乏想象力。
联想词汇	maginative [iˈmædʒinətiv] a. 富于想象力的 imaginary [iˈmædʒinəri] a. 想象中的，虚构的 imaginable [iˈmædʒinəbl] a. 可想象的，可能的	

shame [ʃeim]		
核心词义	n. 羞愧，遗憾的事	Her cheeks glowed with shame. 她面颊羞得发红。 His bad behaviour brings shame on the whole school. 他的恶劣行为使整个学校蒙受耻辱。

拓展词义	v. 使羞愧	The class's unruly behaviour shamed the teacher. 这班学生不守规矩的行为使老师感到羞愧。
习惯用法	put sb. / sth. to shame 使蒙耻辱，使羞愧	
联想词汇	ashamed [əˈʃeimd] a. 惭愧的，害臊的	

hitchhike [ˈhitʃhaik]

核心词义	v. 搭便车旅行	From there, he hitchhiked to Paris in a lorry. 他从那里又搭上了卡车去巴黎。
联想词汇	hitch [hitʃ] v. 猛拉，系住，钩住 n. 猛拉，急推 hike [haik] n. 徒步旅行，远足 v.（口）提高（价格等）	

meantime [ˈmiːnˈtaim]

核心词义	n. 其时，其间	Please find a taxi, and in the meantime I'll pack some food. 请你叫辆出租汽车，趁这功夫我包上些食物。
拓展词义	ad. 与此同时	I continued working, meantime, he went out shopping. 我继续工作，这期间他出去买东西。
词根词缀	mean 在……中间 + time 时间	
习惯用法	in the meantime（meanwhile）在这期间，这时	

lorry [ˈlɔri]

核心词义	n. 卡车，运货汽车	The maximum load for this lorry is one ton. 这辆卡车最大载重量是 1 吨。

border [ˈbɔːdə]

核心词义	n. 边缘	Our garden is bordered on one side by a stream. 我们的花园有一边以小河为界。
习惯用法	on the border of 在……的边界上 border on 与……接壤（相邻）	
联想词汇	boundary [ˈbaundəri] n. 分界线，边界 frontier [ˈfrʌntjə] n. 边界，边境	

词语辨析	boundary，border，frontier 含有边界的意思。 boundary 指边界线，主要指领土的边界； border 指边界，常指边境，即两国边界的地区； frontier 指就一国讲的边界。

evade [i'veid]

核心词义	v. 规避，逃避，躲避	If you try to evade paying your taxes you risk going to prison. 如果你试图逃税，你就有坐牢的危险了。

Lesson

74

Out of the limelight
舞台之外

limelight ['laim,lait]		
核心词义	n. 舞台灯光，众人注目的中心	I hated the limelight and found it unbearable. 我讨厌惹人注目，觉得那实在令人难以忍受。

precaution [pri'kɔ:ʃən]		
核心词义	n. 预防措施，留心，警戒	I took the precaution of locking money in the safe. 我把所有的钱都锁在保险箱里以防万一。
联想词汇	caution ['kɔ:ʃən] n. 小心，慎重，警示	

fan [fæn]		
核心词义	n. 狂热者，迷	My sister is a loyal movie fan. 我妹妹是个忠实的影迷。
拓展词义	n. 风扇	I have a small fan on my desk. 我的书桌上有个小风扇。

shady ['ʃeidi]		
核心词义	a. 成荫的，遮荫的，阴暗的	This is a shady avenue. 这是条林阴大道。
拓展词义	a. 可疑的，靠不住的	He has engaged in rather shady occupation. 他从事相当不明不白的职业。
联想词汇	shadow ['ʃædəu] n. 阴影，影子；虚幻的事物 shed [ʃed] n. 车棚，小屋 vt. 流下，蜕皮，落叶	

sheriff [ˈʃerif]		
核心词义	n. 司法长官；州长	He was appointed Sheriff of New York. 他被任命为纽约司法长官。

notice [ˈnəutis]		
核心词义	n. 告示	Do you understand this notice? 你能看懂这个通知吗？
联想词汇	noticeable [ˈnəutisəbl] a. 显而易见的；引人注意的	

sneer [sniə]		
核心词义	n. 冷笑，嘲笑	He said with a sneer. 他的话中带有嘲笑之意。
拓展词义	v. 讥笑，冷笑	You may sneer, but a lot of people like this kind of music. 你可以嗤之以鼻，但很多人喜欢这种音乐。
习惯用法	sneer at 蔑视，嘲笑	

Lesson

75

SOS
呼救信号

---

thick [θik]

核心词义	a. 厚的；粗的，稠密的	She was still wearing her thick coat. 她还穿着那件厚外套。
拓展词义	a. 粘稠的；不清楚的	Grandfather spoke with a thick Scottish accent. 祖父说话带有很重的苏格兰土腔。

---

signal ['signl]

核心词义	n. 信号，导火线；动机；标志	Signals are made with flags or lamps. 用旗或灯传递信号。
拓展词义	v. 发信号，标志着 a. 显著的	This is a signal failure. 这是明显的失败。
词语辨析	signal 和 sign 都有信号，标号的意思。 signal 是指传递信息的、体现为特殊声音或动态模式的信号； sign 是指有特定意义的象征性符号、标记、有指示作用的标志物或者招牌。	
词根词缀	sign 符号，记号 + -al 名词后缀	

---

stamp [stæmp]

核心词义	v. 在……盖章，贴邮票于……；踩，踩	They stamped the soil flat. 他们把地踏平了。

拓展词义	*n*. 印花，邮票；踩脚	None is genuine without our stamp. 未盖我们戳记的都不是真货。 He gave a stamp of impatience. 他不耐烦地踩脚。
习惯用法	stamp sth. on 在……上盖印，留下印记 stamp down 踩扁，践踏	

helicopter ['helikɔptə]

核心词义	*n*. 直升飞机	The helicopter hovered above us. 直升飞机在我们头上盘旋。

scene [siːn]

核心词义	*n*. 场，景，情景	They have added a new scene at the beginning. 在开头他们又增加了一场戏。 We climbed higher so that we might see the scenes better. 我们又往高处爬以便能更好地观看这景色。
联想词汇	scenery ['siːnəri] *n*. 风景	

survivor [sə'vaivə]

核心词义	*n*. 幸存者	There was only one survivor of the plane crash. 这次飞机失事中只有一名幸存者。
联想词汇	survive [sə'vaiv] *v*. 幸存，活下来；比……活的长 survival [sə'vaivəl] *n*. 生存，幸存	

Lesson

76

April Fools' Day
愚人节

---

fool [fuːl]

核心词义	*n.* 愚人，傻瓜	A fool may give a wise man counsel. 愚者千虑，必有一得。
拓展词义	*v.* 愚弄，欺骗	He felt that he had been deliberately fooled by that man. 他当时觉得那个人故意捉弄了他。

---

bulletin [ˈbulitin]

核心词义	*n.* 公报，新闻快报，期刊	Here is the latest bulletin about the President's health. 这是总统健康情况的最新报告。
联想词汇	bullet [ˈbulit] *n.* 子弹 bully [ˈbuli] *v.* 威胁，恐吓 *n.* 欺凌弱小者	

---

announcer [əˈnaunsə]

核心词义	*n.* （电视、电台）播音员	She is an announcer in TV broadcast. 她是电视台的一名主持人。
联想词汇	announce [əˈnauns] *v.* 发表，广播（电台节目），通告，正式宣布 pronounce [prəˈnauns] *v.* 发音，宣告，断言	

---

macaroni [ˌmækəˈrəuni]

核心词义	*n.* 通心粉，空心面条	He sat down to eat a great dish of macaroni. 他坐下来吃了一大碗通心粉。

leading [ˈliːdɪŋ]

核心词义	a. 领导的，主要的，在前的	She is one of the leading writers of her days. 她是那个时代主要的作家之一。
拓展词义	n. 领导，引导	She was dressed by a leading world designer. 她穿着世界杰出设计师设计的服装。
联想词汇	leader [ˈliːdə] n. 领袖，领导者 leadership [ˈliːdəʃip] n. 领导 mislead [misˈliːd] v. 带错路，使误解，使误入歧途	

grower [ˈɡrəuə(r)]

核心词义	n. 栽培者，种植者	We all know how to plant vegetables for my father was once a vegetable grower. 我们都知道怎么种菜，因为爸爸曾经是菜农。
联想词汇	growth [ɡrəuθ] n. 增长，生长，发育，扩大	

splendid [ˈsplendid]

核心词义	a. 极好的，壮丽的，辉煌的	He got a splendid present for her. 他送她一件极好的礼物。

stalk [stɔːk]

核心词义	n. 茎，梗	She trimmed the stalks of the tulips before putting them in a vase. 她在把郁金香插进花瓶之前修剪了花茎。
拓展词义	v. 大踏步走	She refused to accept that she was wrong and stalked furiously out of the room. 她拒绝承认她错了，气愤地大步走出房间。

gather [ˈɡæðə]

核心词义	v. 收（庄稼）	The villagers are busy on gathering the crop. 村民们正在忙于收庄稼。

thresh [θreʃ]

核心词义	v. 打（庄稼）；脱粒	Farmers thresh grain with threshing machines. 农民用脱粒机脱粒。

process [prə'ses]

核心词义	v. 加工，处理	The factory processes leather. 这个厂加工皮革。
拓展词义	n. 过程，方法，程序，步骤	Adolescence is the process of going from childhood to maturity. 青春期是从少年到成年的过渡期。
联想词汇	proceed [prə'si:d] v. 着手进行，继续进行 procession [prə'seʃən] n. 队伍，行列 procedure [prə'si:dʒə] n. 程序，手续，步骤	

present ['preznt]

核心词义	a. 目前的	He judged the present situation badly. 他很糟糕地错估了当前形势。

champion ['tʃæmpjən]

核心词义	n. 冠军，拥护者	The little girl presented the champion with a victory garland. 小女孩给冠军献上了胜利的花环。
联想词汇	campaign [kæm'pein] n. 战役，运动，活动 v. 参加活动，参加竞选	

studio ['stju:diəu]

核心词义	n. 播音室（工作场所），画室	They are building a modern studio. 他们正在修建一座现代化的摄影室。

Lesson

77

A successful operation
一例成功的手术

mummy [ˈmʌmi]		
核心词义	n. 木乃伊	There will be an Egyptian mummy show in that country. 那个国家将要展示埃及木乃伊。

Egyptian [iˈdʒipʃ(ə)n]		
核心词义	n. 埃及人 a. 埃及的	The ancient Egyptians had advanced civilization. 古埃及人曾经拥有高度文明。
联想词汇	Egypt [ˈiːdʒipt] n. 埃及	

temple [ˈtempl]		
核心词义	n. 庙宇，寺院	Many temples were beautifully built. 许多寺庙建得很美。

mark [mɑːk]		
核心词义	n. 标志，分数，马克，斑点	The spilt coffee has left a mark on the table cloth. 洒出来的咖啡在桌布上留下了印渍。 Command of the mother tongue is the most distinguishing mark of the educated man or woman. 运用本国语言的能力是受过教育的人最明显的标志。
拓展词义	v. 做标记于……，打分数	The table marks very easily. 这张桌子很容易留下印痕。

习惯用法	mark down 记下，减价 mark out 划线分出

plate [pleit]

核心词义	n.（照相）底片	We have succeeded in getting these plates. 我们成功获得了这些底片。
拓展词义	n. 盘，盆，碟	Our host was very generous, heaping a plate of food to us. 主人十分慷慨，给我们装了一盘食物。
习惯用法	a plate of food 一盘食物 in one's plate 心情很好 out of one's plate 心情不好	

disease [di'zi:z]

核心词义	n. 疾病（具体的一种病）	Disease is usually caused by germs. 疾病通常是由病菌引起的。
词根词缀	dis- 不 + ease 舒适	

last [lɑːst]

核心词义	v. 延续，持续；耐用；经受住	I expected the cease-fire to last. 我指望停火会持久。 A pack of cigarettes lasts him two days. 一包香烟够他抽两天的。
拓展词义	a. 最后的，末尾的，最近的，最终的 n. 最后的人或物 ad. 上一次；最后	I received your last letter in May. 我收到你的最近来信是在五月份。 These are the last of our apples. 我们就剩下这么多苹果了。 He came last in the race. 他在赛跑比赛中跑了最后一名。
联想词汇	latter ['lætə] a. 后面的，后者的 lately ['leitli] ad. 最近，不久前 later ['leitə] ad. 较晚地，后来	

prove [pruːv]

核心词义	v. 显示出；证明，查验	Time will prove me to be right. 时间会证明我是对的。
习惯用法	prove that... 证明是…… prove to 向……证明	
联想词汇	approve [əˈpruːv] v. 赞同，核准，证实 improve [imˈpruːv] v. 改良，改善，增进，提高	
词根词缀	词根 prove 表示"证实、验证"的含义	

resin [ˈrezin]

核心词义	n. 树脂	The basin is made of synthetic resin. 这个盆是用合成树脂做的。
联想词汇	resign [riˈzain] v. 辞职，放弃，使顺从	

skin [skin]

核心词义	n. 皮肤，外皮；兽皮	I was caught in a shower of rain and soaked to the skin. 我正赶上一场雨，浑身湿透了。
联想词汇	skim [skim] v. 掠过，略读，省略	

section [ˈsekʃən]

核心词义	n. 部分，章节；部门；路段，地区；切片，剖面	This illustration shows a vertical section through the locust. 本图所示为蝗虫的纵剖面。 A Reading Practice section is added to each unit in Book Two. 在第二册书里每个单元都加上了阅读练习部分。
联想词汇	sector [ˈsektə] n. 扇形，扇区；部门，领域；防御地区	

figure [ˈfigə]

核心词义	n. （人的）体形和形状；图形，数字	I made out three figures moving in the distance. 我隐约看出远处有三个人影在移动。

		The figure on page 22 shows a political map of Africa. 第 22 页的插图是非洲的政区图。
拓展词义	*v*. 演算，认为，领会到	Figure the total and I'll pay it with a cheque. 请把总数算出来，我用支票支付。 I figured that you wouldn't come. 我料想你不会来。

normally [ˈnɔːməli]

核心词义	*ad*. 正常地	Let's face it，people who have a capacity for work normally succeed. 不管怎么说，有工作能力的人一般总会成功的。

survive [səˈvaiv]

核心词义	*v*. 幸存，活下来	These plants cannot survive in very cold conditions. 这些植物在严寒中不能存活。
拓展词义	*v*. 比……活的长	Most parents expect that their children will survive them. 大多数父母都希望子女能够比他们自己长寿。

Lesson

78

The last one?
最后一枝吗？

entitle [in'taitl]		
核心词义	v. 给予……称号，以……为名，使有……权利	This ticket entitles you to a free lunch. 凭此券你可免费吃一顿午餐。
习惯用法	be entitled to sth. 对……享有权利 be entitled 叫做，称为，题目是	
联想词汇	title ['taitl] n. 头衔，名称，标题 entail [in'teil] vt. 使必需，使蒙受，使承担	

calm [kɑːm]		
核心词义	v. 使镇定，使平静	Presently he calmed a little. 他很快就平静一些了。
拓展词义	a. 平静的，冷静的，心平气和的	The sea is now calm. 海现在平静了。
习惯用法	calm down 使平息，使平静	
词语辨析	calm, peaceful, quiet 都含平静的意思。 calm 主要用于气候、海洋风平浪静的，也可指人表示安静的、镇静的； peaceful 指和平的，表示没有骚扰和战争的； quiet 指没有吵闹声的、没有噪音的，它强调声音很低、很少或全然无声。		

nerve [nəːv]

核心词义	n. 神经，胆量，勇气	You'll need plenty of nerve to sit beside him when he is driving. 他开车的时候，你得有足够的胆量才敢坐在他旁边。

concentration [ˌkɔnsen'treiʃən]

核心词义	n. 集中，专心	Large concentrations of capital were in the hands of merchants. 大量资本集中在商人手里。

suffer ['sʌfə]

核心词义	v. 遭受，忍受；受苦，受害	He suffered the humiliation of being forced to resign. 他蒙受了被迫辞职的羞辱。 He could not suffer criticism. 他不能忍受别人批评他。

symptom ['simptəm]

核心词义	n. 症状，征候，征兆	The symptoms manifested themselves ten days later. 十天后征兆显露出来了。

temper ['tempə]

核心词义	n. 脾气，特征，趋向	She has a naturally sweet temper. 她生性和蔼可亲。
习惯用法	out of temper 生气，发脾气	

appetite ['æpitait]

核心词义	n. 食欲，胃口，欲望	The baby has a good appetite. 这个婴儿食欲很好。
词语辨析	appetite，desire，lust 都含有欲望的意思。 appetite 是指对食物的欲望，胃口； desire 是泛指的欲望； lust 特指贪欲。	

produce [prəˈdjuːs]

核心词义	v. 产生，生产；拿出；制作，创作	He produced his railway ticket when asked to do so. 当验票时，他出示了火车票。 This famous author has produced little in the last few years. 这位著名的作家近几年来作品甚少。
拓展词义	n. 产品，农产品	This is all locally grown produce. 这都是本地农产品。
联想词汇	reproduce [ˌriːprəˈdjuːs] v. 再生，复制，生殖 product [ˈprɔdəkt] n. 产品，成果 production [prəˈdʌkʃən] n. 生产，产品，作品，成果	

urge [əːdʒ]

核心词义	v. 力劝；鼓励；促使；怂恿	She urges me to take steps in the matter at once. 她催促我要马上处理此事。 Your progress will urge us to work hard. 你的进步会促进我们努力学习。
习惯用法	urge... into doing /to do 催促……做	
联想词汇	urgent [ˈəːdʒənt] a. 急迫的，紧要的，紧急的	

satisfaction [ˌsætisˈfækʃən]

核心词义	n. 满意，满足	She laughed her satisfaction. 她以笑表示满意。
联想词汇	satisfactory [ˌsætisˈfæktəri] a. 令人满意的	

delighted [diˈlaitid]

核心词义	a. 高兴的，欣喜的	I'm delighted at your success. 我为你的成功感到高兴。

词语辨析	pleasure，delight，joy 都含快乐、愉快的意思。 pleasure 是常用词，指以任何形式表现出的或默默的快乐与满足； delight 语意比 pleasure 强，指极大的快乐，尤指以一种活泼的态度表现出来的快乐； joy 指高兴地表现出来的更强烈的快乐和愉快的情绪。

Lesson 79

By air
乘飞机

parent [ˈpɛərənt]

核心词义	n. 父母亲	As an only child he was the idol of his parents. 作为独子，他是父母的宠儿。

flight attendant [ˈflait-əˈtendənt]

核心词义	空中乘务员	I asked the flight attendant to bring me some coffee. 我请空服员给我一些咖啡。

frightened [ˈfrait(ə)nd]

核心词义	a. 受惊的，受恐吓的	The child is frightened of dogs. 这孩子怕狗。

curious [ˈkjuəriəs]

核心词义	a. 好奇的，古怪的	The boy was curious about everything he saw. 那男孩对所见的一切都感到好奇。
习惯用法	be curious about sth. 对（某事物）感到好奇 be curious to (do) 很想（做）；渴望（做）	
联想词汇	curiosity [ˌkjuəriˈɔsiti] n. 好奇，好奇心	

bomb [bɔm]

核心词义	n. 炸弹	His one leg was blown off by a bomb in the war. 他的一条腿在战争中被炸弹炸掉了。
拓展词义	v. 轰炸，投弹于	Terrorists bombed several police stations. 恐怖分子炸毁了几所警察局。

plant [plɑːnt]		
核心词义	v. 安放	They must have planted many explosives there. 他们一定在这里埋了很多炸药。

Lesson

80

The Crystal Palace
水晶宫

---

palace [ˈpælis]

核心词义	n. 宫殿	Have you been to the Imperial Palace? 你去过故宫吗?
联想词汇	place [pleis] n. 地方，场所，某处，位置，等级，职位 v. 放置，安排 displace [disˈpleis] v. 移置，替换 replace [ri(:)ˈpleis] vt. 取代，替换，代替，把……放回原处	

extraordinary [ikˈstrɔːdənəri]

核心词义	a. 不平常的，非凡的	A trunk is extraordinary long! 象的鼻子特别的长!

exhibition [ˌeksiˈbiʃən]

核心词义	n. 展览，展览会	She will have an exhibition of her pictures. 她将为自己的画作举办一个展览会。
拓展词义	n. 表现，显示	The quiz was a good opportunity for the exhibition of his knowledge. 这次测验是他显示知识的好机会。

iron [ˈaiən]

核心词义	n. 铁，熨斗	This basin is made of iron. 这个盆子是铁做的。

拓展词义	v. 熨平	She's been ironing all afternoon. 她一下午都在熨衣服。

various ['vɛəriəs]

核心词义	a. 各种各样的	The products we sell are many and various. 我们出售的产品是各式各样的。
联想词汇	vary ['vɛəri] vt. 使变化，改变 variable ['vɛəriəbl] a. 可变的，易变的 variety [və'raiəti] n. 多样，种类，多样化 variation [ˌvɛəri'eiʃən] n. 变化，变动，变种，变异	

machinery [mə'ʃiːnəri]

核心词义	n.（总称）机器，机械	A factory contains much machinery. 一家工厂可容纳很多机器。
联想词汇	mechanism ['mekənizəm] n. 机械，机械装备（结构），机构 mechanic [mi'kænik] a. 手工的 n. 技工，机修工 mechanical [mi'kænikl] a. 机械的，力学的，呆板的	

display [di'splei]

核心词义	n. 展览，陈列	A new kind of car was on display in the shop. 商店里展出一种新汽车。
拓展词义	v. 展现，陈列；显示，显露	The young woman proudly displayed her furs. 那个年轻女人骄傲地炫耀她的皮衣。
词语辨析	show，display，exhibit，expose 都含景象的出现或展示某物让人看的意思。 show 属于常用词，指故意或无意给人看所显示之物； display 指把某物展出使人们看到； exhibit 指为出售、竞赛等而陈列； expose 指陈列商品等。	

steam [stiːm]

核心词义	*n.* 蒸汽	The steam sang as it escaped from the pipe. 蒸汽从管子逸出时呜呜作响。

profit ['prɔfit]

核心词义	*n.* 利润，赢利，利益	What's the profit of doing that? 做那件事有什么好处呢？
拓展词义	*v.* 有益，获利，赚钱	Taking these courses profited him. 选修这些课程对他有好处。
习惯用法	profit by/from 从……中得到益处	
词语辨析	profit，behalf 表示利润的时候只能用 profit，其他的时候两者都可以互换。	

college ['kɔlidʒ]

核心词义	*n.* 学院	Our daughter is going to college in autumn. 我们的女儿秋天就要上大学了。
联想词汇	colleague ['kɔliːg] *n.* 同事	

Lesson 81

Escape
脱逃

prisoner [ˈprɪznə]		
核心词义	n. 囚犯	Two prisoners have escaped. 有两个囚犯逃走了。

bush [buʃ]		
核心词义	n. 灌木， 灌木丛	There is a bush near the school playground. 学校操场附近有一片灌木丛。

rapidly [ˈræpɪdli]		
核心词义	ad. 迅速地	He was rapidly leaving the others behind. 他迅速地把其他人甩在后面。

uniform [ˈjuːnɪfɔːm]		
核心词义	n. 制服	The new uniforms will arrive tomorrow. 新制服明天就到。
拓展词义	a. 一致的， 统一的	The earth turns around at a uniform rate. 地球以相同的速度旋转。
词根词缀	词根 uni- + -form 形式 = 被统一在一种形式里的东西	

rifle [ˈraɪfl]		
核心词义	n. 来福枪， 步枪	They have a few rifles. 他们有几支步枪。

shoulder [ˈʃəʊldə]		
核心词义	n. 肩膀	I feel a dull ache in the shoulder. 我的肩膀感到隐约疼痛。

| 拓展词义 | *v.* 扛，挑 | The boy shouldered a basket of fruits. 这个男孩扛了一筐水果。 |
| 习惯用法 | shoulder to shoulder 肩并肩地，同心协力地 | |

march [mɑːtʃ]

| 核心词义 | *v.* 行进，前进 | The crowd of demonstrators marched along the main street. 游行群众沿主要街道行进。 |

boldly ['bəuldli]

| 核心词义 | *ad.* 大胆地，显眼地 | Jane walked boldly up to the platform without faltering. 简沉着大胆地走上讲台。 |

blaze [bleiz]

| 核心词义 | *v.* 猛烈的燃烧，发光 | Lights were blazing in every room. 每个房间都灯火通明。 |
| 拓展词义 | *n.* 火焰，烈火 | Dry wood makes a good blaze. 干木燃起夺目的光焰。 |

salute [sə'luːt]

| 核心词义 | *v./n.* 敬礼，欢迎，致敬 | The guard saluted me smartly. 卫兵向我行了个漂亮的军礼。 The Queen's birthday was honoured by a 21-gun salute. 鸣21响礼炮庆祝女王的生日。 |
| 联想词汇 | salvation [sæl'veiʃən] *n.* 得救，拯救 | |

elderly ['eldəli]

| 核心词义 | *a.* 上了中年的，稍老的 | The elderly man is quite energetic. 这位上了年纪的老人仍精力充沛。 |

grey ［grei］

核心词义	a. 灰色的，灰白的	He wore a grey suit. 他穿一套灰衣服。
拓展词义	n. 灰色	This colour is grey. 这种颜色是灰色。

sharp ［ʃɑːp］

核心词义	a. 刺耳的；锋利的；急剧的，猛烈的；明显的；严厉的	The famous writer is still sharp in thought though he is so old. 这位著名作家年事已高，但仍然思维敏捷。There is a sharp bend in the road. 路上有一个急转弯。She got a sharp reproach from her boss. 她受到了上司的严厉训斥。
拓展词义	ad. 准时地，突然地	Please be on hand at 12 sharp. 请在 12 点整到这里来。

blow ［bləu］

核心词义	n. 打击，一击	He gave him a violent blow on the head. 他照他的头部重重一击。
拓展词义	v. (blew；blown) 吹，风吹；吹响；使爆炸	The fan was blowing. 风扇正吹着。The balloon has blown. 气球炸开了。
习惯用法	blow off 离开，离去blow out 使熄灭blow up 爆炸；打气	

Lesson

82

Monster or fish?
是妖还是鱼？

---

monster [ˈmɔnstə]		
核心词义	n. 怪物，恶人，巨物	This is a horrible monster. 这是一个可怕的怪物。
拓展词义	a. 巨大的，庞大的	Many monster high-rise buildings spring up all over the city. 许多巨大的高层建筑在这座城市拔地而起。

sailor [ˈseilə]		
核心词义	n. 海员，水手	In the after years the sailor did not get home often. 在往后的几年里这个水手经常不回家。

sight [sait]		
核心词义	v. 见到	After five days at sea, we sighted land. 我们在海上航行了 5 天后见到了陆地。

creature [ˈkriːtʃə]		
核心词义	v. 见到	The crocodile is a strange-looking creature. 鳄鱼是一种模样古怪的动物。
联想词汇	creative [kri(ː)ˈeitiv] a. 创造性的 recreation [rekriˈeiʃ(ə)n] n. 消遣，娱乐	

peculiar [piˈkjuːliə]		
核心词义	a. 奇怪的，古怪的，特殊的，独特的	The wine has a peculiar taste. 这种酒有种怪怪的味道。 The book has a peculiar value. 这本书有特殊的价值。

联想词汇	particular [pə'tikjulə] *a.* 特别的，独有的，挑剔的
	particle ['pɑ:tikl] *n.* 粒子，颗粒

shining ['ʃainiŋ]

核心词义	*a.* 闪闪发光的，华丽的	What shiny shoes you're wearing!
		你穿的鞋子擦得真亮啊!

oarfish ['ɔ:fiʃ]

核心词义	*n.* 桨鱼	We never seen oarfish before.
		我们之前从没看过桨鱼。

Lesson

83

After the election
大选之后

---

election [i'lekʃ(ə)n]

核心词义	n. 选举	Charles declared the result of the election. 查尔斯宣布了选举结果。
联想词汇	selection [si'lekʃən] n. 选择，挑选	

---

former ['fɔːmə]

核心词义	a. 以前的，在前的	Some of them bitterly attacked their former friends. 他们中有些人恶毒地攻击他们过去的朋友。

---

defeat [di'fiːt]

核心词义	v. 击败；战胜；使困惑	Our football team defeated theirs this time. 这一次我们的足球队胜了他们的足球队。 This kind of problems always defeats me. 我总是无法应付这类问题。
拓展词义	n. 战胜，挫败	They had two defeats this year. 他们今年都失败两次了。

---

fanatical [fə'nætikəl]

核心词义	a. 狂热的	She's fanatical about keeping fit. 她如痴如醉地注重自己的体形。

opponent [əˈpəunənt]

核心词义	*n.* 对手，敌手，反对者	He beat his opponent in the election. 他在选举中击败了对手。

radical [ˈrædikəl]

核心词义	*a.* 根本的；激进的；彻底的	The patient got a radical cure in the hospital. 病人在医院得到了根治。

progressive [prəˈgresiv]

核心词义	*a.* 进步的，前进的；发展的	This is a progressive course in English study. 这是英语学习的渐进课程。
联想词汇	aggressive [əˈgresiv] *a.* 侵犯的，攻击性的，有进取心的	

ex- [eks]

核心词义	*prefix.*（前缀，用于名词前）前…… This is a progressive course in English study. 这是英语学习的渐进课程。
联想词汇	anti- [ˈænti] *prefix.* 反……，阻…… mis- [mis] *prefix.* 坏、错；缺乏，相反 multi- [mʌlti] *prefix.* 多 non- [nuŋ] *prefix.* 非，不 il- [il] *prefix.* 否定 im- [ˈim] *prefix.*（用于 b, m 或 p 前）不，非 semi- [semi] *prefix.* 一半的；部分的，不完全的 sub- [sʌb] *prefix.* 在……之下，低于；次于；（地位）低，副 trans- [ˈtræns] *prefix.* 横过，到……的另一边

suspicious [səsˈpiʃəs]

核心词义	*a.* 怀疑的，可疑的，疑心的	The rabbit is timid and suspicious. 兔子胆小而多疑。 The police are suspicious of his alibi because he already has a record. 警方对他不在场的辩解表示怀疑，因为他已有前科。

Lesson

84

On strike
罢工

strike [straik]		
核心词义	*n*. 罢工，攻击	The dockers are striking. 码头工人正在罢工。
拓展词义	*v*.（struck；struck， stricken）攻击， 袭击，突然发 现……，突然 出现在（某人 的脑海中）	They have struke a heavy blow at the aggressors. 他们给侵略者沉 痛的打击。 As I watched them, an idea struck me. 我看着他们时，产生了一个 想法。
习惯用法	strike off 删去，涂去，扣除，除去 be on strike 举行罢工 strike on/upon 打在……上，撞在……上 突然想到或发现 It strikes me that 我觉得……，留给我的印象是……	

busman ['bʌsmən]		
核心词义	*n*. 公共汽 车司机	The busman stopped the bus. 公共汽车司机停下了车。

state [steit]		
核心词义	*v*. 说，陈述， 声明	He stated his problem clearly. 他把问题叙述得很清楚。
拓展词义	*n*. 州，国，状 态，情形	Air whether in the gaseous or liquid state is a fluid. 空气，无论是气态的 或是液态的，都是一种流体。 In America, the law varies from state to state. 美国各州的法律都不同。

习惯用法	state of mind 心境，心情；思想（精神）状态
词语辨析	state，condition，situation 含情况的意思。 state 属于常用词，指人或物存在或所处的状态，但不着重强调这种状态和具体原因或条件的关系； condition 指由于一定的原因、条件或环境所产生的特定情况； situation 指多种具体情况造成的综合状态，主要强调这种状态的影响或处于该状态的事物的关系。

agreement [əˈɡriːmənt]

核心词义	n. 协议；同意	It took three years for the two countries to hammer out an agreement. 两国花了 3 年的时间经过反复讨论才达成协议。
习惯用法	in agreement with 符合……，照……，同意，（和）……一致 make an agreement with 与……达成协议	

relieve [riˈliːv]

核心词义	v. 减轻，救济，解除	The doctors did their best to relieve the patient. 医生们尽力减轻病人的痛苦。
习惯用法	relieve sb. of sth. 解除某人的负担	

pressure [ˈpreʃə(r)]

核心词义	v. 减轻，救济，解除	We must bring pressure in him. 我们应对他施加压力。
拓展词义	n. 强制，压迫	He changed his mind under the pressure from others. 他在别人的逼迫之下改变了主意。
习惯用法	press 压 + -ure 名词后缀	

extent [iks'tent]

核心词义	*n*. 广度，宽度，长度；大小，范围；程度	The new race track is nearly six miles in extent. 这条新跑道将近 6 英里长。 What's the extent of the damage? 损坏的强度如何？
联想词汇	extend [iks'tend] *v*. 扩充，延伸，伸展，扩展	
习惯用法	to some extent 在一定程度上	

volunteer [vɔlən'tiə(r)]

核心词义	*n*. 志愿者	He works as a volunteer at off time. 在业余时间，他从事志愿者工作。
拓展词义	*v*. 自愿提出，自愿	How many of them volunteered? 他们当中有多少人愿意自愿效劳？

gratitude ['grætitjuːd]

核心词义	*n*. 感谢，感激	Her eyes were immediately filled with gratitude. 她的眼里立刻充满了感激之情。
联想词汇	attitude ['ætitjuːd] *n*. 态度，看法，姿势 altitude ['æltitjuːd] *n*. 高度，海拔 latitude ['lætitjuːd] *n*. 纬度 longitude ['lɔndʒitjuːd] *n*. 经度	

Press [pres]

核心词义	*n*. 新闻界	The Press have / has been invited to a press conference to hear the government's statement on the event. 新闻记者已应邀参加新闻发布会，听取政府关于这一事件的声明。

object [ˈɔbdʒikt]

核心词义	v. 反对，不赞成	They objected that the plan was risky. 他们反对说，这项计划是冒险的。
拓展词义	n. 物，物体，目标，宾语	Our object is to get at the truth. 我们的目的是弄清事实真相。 What are those strange objects? 那些奇异物体是什么？
词根词缀	词根-ject 表示"投"的含义。例如：inject [inˈdʒekt] v. 注射，注入	
联想词汇	reject [riˈdʒekt] vt. 拒绝，驳回，丢弃 subject [ˈsʌbdʒikt] n. 科目，主题 v. 使……服从，屈服	

Lesson

85

Never too old to learn
活到老学到老

---

inform [in'fɔːm]

核心词义	v. 通知，告诉，向……报告	We can be informed of a lot by reading books. 通过阅读书籍我们可以了解很多东西。
拓展词义	v. 检举，告发	They decided to inform against him. 他们决定告发他。
习惯用法	inform sb. of sth. 通知某人某事 be informed of 听说，了解；接到……的通知	
联想词汇	transform [træns'fɔːm] v. 改变 reform [ri'fɔːm] v. 改革，改过自新，改善 n. 改革，改正	
词根词缀	in 在……内 + form 形状；在心里造成形状就引申为通知	

---

headmaster [hed'mɑːstə(r)]

核心词义	n. 校长	The headmaster is marking the papers. 校长正给考卷评分数。

---

contribute [kən'tribjuːt]

核心词义	v. 有助于，捐助；投稿；贡献	Everyone was asked to contribute suggestions for the party. 要求每一个人都要为晚会出主意。 I contributed a pound towards Jane's leaving present. 我凑了 1 英镑给简买告别礼物。

习惯用法	contribute to 贡献，捐助……
联想词汇	tribute ['tribjuːt] *n*. 贡品，颂词，称赞 attribute [ə'tribju(ː)t] *n*. 属性，特征 　　　　　　　　*vt*. 把……归因于…… distribute [dis'tribju(ː)t] *vt*. 分配，散布，散播
词根词缀	词根-tribute 表示"给、给予"的含义

gift [gift]

核心词义	*n*. 礼物，赠品， 天赋	I neglected to bring a gift. 我忘了带一件礼物来。
习惯用法	have a gift for 对……有天赋	
词语辨析	gift，present 都含礼物的意思。 gift 在语体上较为正式，带有一定的感情色彩，侧重送礼人的诚意，有时含有捐赠的意思； present 属于普通用语，一般指值钱不多的礼物，表示下对上送礼的意思。	

album ['ælbəm]

核心词义	*n*. 集邮本，照 册，签名簿， 唱片簿	The photos belong in an album. 这些照片应该放在相册里。

patience ['peiʃəns]

核心词义	*n*. 耐心	We haven't the patience to hear such an empty talk. 我们可没耐心去听这种空谈。

encouragement [in'kʌridʒmənt]

核心词义	*n*. 鼓励	They attribute their success to their teacher's encouragement. 他们把成功归因于老师的鼓励。
联想词汇	discourage [dis'kʌridʒ] *vt*. 使气馁，使失去信心	

farewell [ˈfeəˈwel]		
核心词义	n. 告别	He made his farewell to his family. 他向他的家人告别。
联想词汇	welfare [ˈwelfɛə] n. 福利，社会保障 fare [fɛə] n. 费用，食物 vi. 进展；进食	
词根词缀	fare（祈使语气）＋well 好，美满	

honour [ˈɒnə(r)]		
核心词义	n. 光荣；尊敬，敬意	Her honour was discredited in the newspapers. 她的名声被报纸败坏了。 It has been a great honour your coming to visit me. 您来看我是我莫大的荣幸。
拓展词义	v. 尊敬	We all honour courageous people. 我们都尊重勇敢的人。

coincidence [kəuˈinsidəns]		
核心词义	n. 巧合，符合，一致	She and I both arrived at the same time by pure coincidence. 我和她同时到达纯属巧合。

total [ˈtəutl]		
核心词义	n. 总计	A total of twenty people were killed. 共有 20 人被杀。
拓展词义	a. 全体的，总的；完全的 v. 计算	Please figure out the total cost. 请算出总费用。 Please total all the expenditures. 请计算一下全部支出是多少。

devote [diˈvəut]		
核心词义	v. 投入于，致力于，献身	He devoted all his time to his job. 他把他的全部时间都用在工作上了。

习惯用法	devote to 把……献给；把……专用于
	devote oneself to 致力于，献身于；专心于
联想词汇	vote [vəut] n. 投票，表决 v. 投票，选举

gardening ['gɑːdniŋ]

核心词义	n. 园艺	I received a set of gardening tools on my birthday. 生日那天，我收到一套园艺工具。
联想词汇	kingdergarten ['kindəˌgɑːtn] n. 幼儿园	
	gardener ['gɑːdnə(r)] n. 园丁，花匠，园艺家	

hobby ['hɔbi]

核心词义	n. 业余爱好，嗜好	He entered into politics as a hobby. 他参加政治活动是作为一种业余爱好。

Lesson

86

Out of control
失控

---

swing [swiŋ]

核心词义	v. (swung, swung) 使突然转向	The value of the pound swung downwards. 英镑的价值突然下跌。
拓展词义	v. 摇摆，使……旋转 n. 摇摆，改变	He swung the axe and with one blow split open the door. 他挥动着斧子一下就把门劈开了。

---

speedboat ['spi:dbəut]

核心词义	n. 快艇	The man tried to swing the speedboat round. 那人试图让快艇转弯。

---

desperately ['despəritli]

核心词义	ad. 拼命地，极严重地，失望地	We desperately need that money. 我们确实非常需要那笔钱。

---

companion [kəm'pænjən]

核心词义	n. 同伴，同事	His brother is not much of a companion for him. 他兄弟与他情趣不甚相投。

---

water ski ['wɔ:tə-ski:]

核心词义	n. 滑水（由快艇牵引水橇）	My son could water ski for 1 hour. 我儿子能坚持滑水 1 小时。

buoy [bɔi]

核心词义	n. 浮标；救生衣	We tie up at that large red buoy. 我们把船系在那个红色的大浮筒上。
拓展词义	v. 使浮起，支撑，维持	The raft was buoyed up by empty petrol cans. 这木筏依靠空汽油桶的浮力漂浮。
联想词汇	buoyancy ['bɔiənsi] n. 浮力	

dismay [dis'mei]

核心词义	n. 惊愕，气馁，沮丧	I am filled with dismay at the news. 我对这个消息极为震惊。
拓展词义	v. 使……惊愕，失望，泄气	He was dismayed at his lack of understanding. 他对自己的无知感到沮丧。

tremendous [tri'mendəs]

核心词义	a. 巨大的，惊人的	There is a tremendous difference between them. 他们之间有着极大的差别。

petrol ['petrəl]

核心词义	n. 汽油	Our car was useless for want of petrol. 由于缺少汽油，我们的汽车派不上用场。
联想词汇	petroleum [pi'trəuliəm] n. 石油	

drift [drift]

核心词义	v. 漂动，漂流，漂泊	The snow drifted everywhere. 雪飘至各处。
拓展词义	n. 漂移；堆积物；倾向	There is a slow drift into crisis. 有一种渐入危机的趋势。
习惯用法	on the drift（船）漂流 drift away（人）渐渐离开；（烟雾等）慢慢散去	

gently [ˈdʒentli]		
核心词义	*ad*. 轻轻地，缓慢地；温柔地	She always speaks gently to the child. 她对孩子说话总是很温和。
联想词汇	gentleman [ˈdʒentlmən] *n*. 绅士，先生	

Lesson

87

A perfect alibi
极好的不在犯罪现场的证据

alibi ['ælibai]

核心词义	*n.* 不在犯罪现场	Do you have any proof to substantiate your alibi? 你有证据表明你当时不在犯罪现场吗?
联想词汇	ability [ə'biliti] *n.* 才能,能力	

commit [kə'mit]

核心词义	*v.* 委托(托付),犯罪,作……事,承诺	She committed herself to philanthropy. 她专心从事慈善事业。
习惯用法	commit oneself to 委身于,专心致志于 commit oneself on 对……表态	
联想词汇	commission [kə'miʃən] *n.* 授权,委托,佣金 committee [kə'miti] *n.* 委员会	

inspector [in'spektə]

核心词义	*n.* 检查员,巡视员;探长	Factory inspector cost on average £25,000 per head per annum. 工厂检查员平均每人每年花25000英镑。

employer [im'plɔiə]

核心词义	*n.* 雇主	The car industry is one of our biggest employers. 汽车工业是我们最大的雇主之一。

confirm [kənˈfɜːm]

核心词义	v. 确定，批准，证实	We have confirmed the report. 我们证实了那则报道。 The king confirmed that the election would be held on July 20th. 国王批准选举在 7 月 20 日举行。

suggest [səˈdʒest]

核心词义	v. 提醒	The sight of birds suggested a new idea for flying machines. 鸟的形象使人产生一个制造航空机的新主意。

truth [truːθ]

核心词义	n. 事实，真相；真理	I'm going to ascertain the truth. 我要查明真相。 He was a seeker for truth. 他是一个追求真理的人。
联想词汇	trust [trʌst] vt. 信任，相信 n. 信任，信赖；托管	
词根词缀	true 真实的 + -th 名词后缀	

Lesson

88

Trapped in a mine
困在矿井里

---

trap [træp]

核心词义	v. 诱骗，使陷入绝境	Thirty miners were trapped underground after the fire. 起火后有 30 名矿工被困在地底下。
拓展词义	n. 圈套，陷阱，计谋	The police set a trap to catch the thief. 警察设下了捉拿窃贼的圈套。

---

surface ['sɜːfis]

核心词义	n. 表面，地面，平面	The boy disturbed the tranquil surface of the pond with a stick. 那男孩用棍子打破了平静的池面。 You must not look only at the surface of things. 看事物不能只看表面现象。
联想词汇	preface ['prefis] n. 序文，绪言，前言	
词根词缀	sur- = super- 在上面 + face 面	

---

explosive [iks'pləusiv]

核心词义	a. 爆炸（性）的，极易引起争论的	A gas pipe was explosive. 一个煤气管爆炸了。
拓展词义	n. 炸药	Dynamite is an explosive. 炸药是爆炸物。

---

vibration [vai'breiʃən]

核心词义	n. 震动，颤动	The vibration of the window woke me up. 窗子的震动把我惊醒了。

collapse [kə'læps]

核心词义	v. 塌下，崩溃	The bridge collapsed under the weight of the train. 桥在火车的重压下塌了。
拓展词义	n. 崩溃，倒塌	He unexpected rainstorm caused the collapse of their roof. 突来的暴风雨把他们的房顶弄塌了。

drill [dril]

核心词义	v. 训练；钻孔，打眼	He used a drill to bore a hole in the door. 他用钻在门上钻孔。
拓展词义	n. 钻头，操练	The dentist drilled my tooth. 牙医在我的牙齿上钻孔。

capsule ['kæpsju:l]

核心词义	n. 胶囊，太空舱；容器	The doctor advised me to take a capsule this morning. 医生建议我今天早晨服一粒胶囊。

layer ['leiə]

核心词义	n. 层	These seeds must be covered with a layer of earth. 这些种子必须盖上一层泥土。
联想词汇	layout ['lei,aut] n. 布局，安排，设计 layoff ['lei,ɔ:f] n. 临时解雇 layman ['leimən] n. 门外汉，外行人	

beneath [bi'ni:θ]

核心词义	prep. 在……之下	They sheltered beneath their umbrellas. 他们躲到了伞下。 Richard is far beneath Henry in intelligence. 理查的智力远不及亨利。
拓展词义	ad. 在下方	Her careful make-up hid the signs of age beneath. 她的精心化妆掩饰了岁月留下的痕迹。

联想词汇	underneath [ˌʌndəˈniːθ] *ad*. 在下面 *prep*. 在……下面 *n*. 下部，底部	

lower [ˈləuə]

核心词义	*v*. 放下，降低；削减，减弱	A cold had lowered her resistance. 感冒已削弱了她的抵抗力。
拓展词义	*a*. 低的，下级的，低等的	The lower classes are always with us. 我们总是和下层社会人民在一起。

progress [ˈprəuges]

核心词义	*v*. 促进，进步，进行	The work is progressing steadily. 工作在稳步地取得进展。
拓展词义	*n*. 进步，发展，前进	Our progress was embarrassed by lots of baggage. 大量的行李使我们行进困难。
习惯用法	in progress 在进行中，在举行 make progress 取得进展，进步 make progress in 在……方面取得进步	
词根词缀	pro- 前向 + 拉丁词根 gress 步，走；由"向前走"而引申为进步	

smoothly [ˈsmuːðli]

核心词义	*ad*. 平滑地，流畅地，流利地	I can speak english smoothly. 我讲英语很流利。

A slip of tougue
口误

slip [slip]

核心词义	n. 滑倒，小过失	One slip and you could fall off the building. 脚下一滑就可能从建筑物上跌下去。
拓展词义	v. 使滑动；摆脱；滑倒，失足；减退	She slipped away without being seen. 她悄悄的溜走，没有被人发现。 The dog slipped its collar and ran away. 那条狗挣脱了项圈逃走了。
联想词汇	slippery ['slipəri] a. 滑的	
习惯用法	slip away 悄悄溜走	

comedy ['kɔmidi]

核心词义	n. 喜剧	Do you prefer comedy or tragedy? 你喜欢喜剧还是悲剧？
联想词汇	tragedy ['trædʒidi] n. 悲剧，惨事，灾难	

present ['preznt]

核心词义	v. 演出 a. 出席，到场的	How many of the group are present today? 今天该组有多少人出席？ The theatre company is presenting 'Romeo and Julia' by Shakespeare next week. 剧团下星期将演出莎士比亚剧"罗密欧和朱丽叶"。

queue [kjuː]		
核心词义	*v.* 排队 *n.* 行列，长队	To what window are you standing in a queue? 你在排哪个窗口的队？
习惯用法	jump the queue 插队	

dull [dʌl]		
核心词义	*a.* 枯燥，无味	His life is so dull. 他的生活很枯燥。
拓展词义	*a.* 钝的，不锋利的；不鲜明的；萧条的	The knife is dull. 那把刀很钝。

artiste [ɑːˈtist]		
核心词义	*n.* 艺人	Is there a guarantee I will be an artiste? 是不是能保证我一定会成为一位艺人？

advertiser [ˈædvətaizə]		
核心词义	*n.* 广告者，广告客户；报幕员	We've had several phone calls already this morning from advertisers. 我们今天上午已接到好几个广告客户的电话。
联想词汇	adverse [ˈædvəːs] *a.* 不利的，有害的，相反的，敌对的 advertisement [ədˈvəːtismənt] *n.* 广告	

Lesson

90

What's for supper?
晚餐吃什么?

chip [tʃip]

核心词义	n. 薄片，芯片；油煎土豆片	Potato chips are served for the children. 给儿童端上炸薯条。
拓展词义	v. 削，切，削成碎片	This china chips easily. 这瓷器很容易碎。
联想词汇	chop [tʃɔp] v. 剁碎，砍，切	
习惯用法	chip off 切下来，削下来	

overfish ['əuvəfiʃ]

核心词义	v. 对（鱼）进行过度捕捞	Never overfish on the sea every year. 每年决不能去海里过度捕捞。

giant ['dʒaiənt]

核心词义	a. 巨大的 n. 巨人	The giant packet gives you more for less money! 特大的包装使你用便宜的价钱买到超值的分量!
联想词汇	gigantic [dʒai'gæntik] a. 巨大的	

terrify ['terifai]

核心词义	v. 使恐怖，吓	That sort of thing terrifies people. 那样的事令人感到恐怖。
习惯用法	be terrify fied of 对……感到恐怖	
联想词汇	terrible ['terəbl] a. 可怕的，严重的，令人震惊的，剧烈的 terror ['terə] n. 恐怖，恐怖活动	

diver ['daivə]

核心词义	n. 潜水员；跳水运动员	The young diver is working under the water with a diving suit. 潜水员穿着潜水衣正在水下工作。

oil-rig [ɔil-rig]

核心词义	n. 石油钻塔	The oil-rig workers are claiming a 12% pay rise. 石油钻井工人要求增加12%的工资。
联想词汇	rig [rig] v. 给（船等）装配帆，给（飞机）装配机翼　装配	

wit [wit]

核心词义	n. 才智；（pl.）理智，头脑	He is a boy of quick wits. 他是一个机敏的孩子。
联想词汇	witness ['witnis] n. 目击者，证人 v. 目击，作证	
词根词缀	词根 vis＝wit 表示看、看见的含义	

cage [keidʒ]

核心词义	n. 笼子	The old man wants to buy a cage for birds. 老人想买一个鸟笼。
拓展词义	v. 把……关入笼内	After the tiger was caught，it was caged. 老虎被捉住后关进了笼子。

shark [ʃɑːk]

核心词义	n. 鲨鱼	They were killed by a man-eating shark. 他们被一条吃人的鲨鱼所害。

whale [weil, hw-]

核心词义	n. 鲸	The blue whale is the world's largest living animal. 蓝鲸是世界上最大的动物。

variety [və'raiəti]

核心词义	n. 多样，种类，多样化	This variety of dog is very useful for hunting. 这种狗对狩猎很有用。

cod [kɔd]

核心词义	n. 鳕鱼	Cod are found in the North Atlantic and the North Sea. 北大西洋和北海有鳕鱼。

skate [skeit]

核心词义	n. 鳐鱼 v. 溜冰，滑冰	She skates beautifully. 她滑冰动作优美。

factor ['fæktə]

核心词义	n. 因素	Industry and modesty are the chief factors of his success. 勤奋和谦虚是他成功的主要因素。
联想词汇	fact [fækt] n. 实际，事实 factory ['fæktəri] n. 工厂 manufacturer [ˌmænju'fæktʃərə] n. 制造商 manufacture [ˌmænju'fæktʃə] n. 产品，制造，制造业 　　　　　　　　　　　　　　　　v. 制造，加工	

crew [kru:]

核心词义	n. 全体船员，全体乘务员	The plane crashed, killing all its passengers and crew. 飞机失事了，所有乘客和机组人员都遇难了。
联想词汇	screw [skru:] n. 螺丝钉，螺旋，压迫 v. 转动，旋，拧	

Lesson

91

Three man in a basket
三人同篮

balloon [bəˈluːn]		
核心词义	*n.* 气球	Many children like balloons. 许多孩子都喜欢气球。

royal [ˈrɔiəl]		
核心词义	*a.* 王室的，皇家的，高贵的	The royal wedding was an occasion of great festivity. 皇室婚礼是喜庆的盛事。

spy [spai]		
核心词义	*n.* 间谍，侦探，侦察	Everybody suspect she is a spy. 大家都怀疑她是个间谍。
拓展词义	*v.* 发现，当间谍	She was accused of spying for the enemy. 她被指控为敌方间谍。

track [træk]		
核心词义	*n.* 轨迹，踪迹	The motorcar tracks is very clear. 汽车的痕迹很明显。
拓展词义	*n.* 小路，小径；跑道 *v.* 跟踪	They passed a muddy track through the forest. 他们穿过森林的泥泞小路。 The police used dogs to track the criminal. 警察用警犬来追踪罪犯。
词语辨析		trace，track 都含留下的痕迹或记号的意思。 trace 指某些已出现或发生的事所留下的记号、痕迹等； track 指车辆、行人、动物等经过后留下的痕迹、踪迹或足迹。

binoculars [bɪˈnɒkjʊləz]

| 核心词义 | n. 双筒望远镜 | He watched the play through his binoculars. 他用双筒望远镜看戏。 |

Lesson

92

Asking for trouble
自找麻烦

fast [fɑːst]		
核心词义	*ad*. 迅速地，紧紧地；熟（睡）	The boat was stuck fast in the mud. 那艘船深深地陷在泥里。
拓展词义	*a*. 快速的，紧紧的，牢固的	She was a fast weaver and the cloth was very good. 她织布织得很快，而且布的质量很好。 Nothing can undermine their fast friendship. 没有什么能破坏他们忠实的友谊。
联想词汇	breakfast ['brekfəst] *n*. 早餐 *v*. 吃早餐；提供……早餐 fasten ['fɑːsn] *vt*. 拴紧，使固定，系	

ladder ['lædə]		
核心词义	*n*. 梯子	The little boy had an unsteady footing on the ladder. 那小孩在梯子上站得不稳。

shed [ʃed]		
核心词义	*n*. 车棚，小屋	He built a bicycle shed. 他盖了一间自行车棚。
拓展词义	*v*. 流下，蜕皮，落叶	Many trees shed their leaves in autumn. 许多树在秋天落叶。

sarcastic [sɑː'kæztik]		
核心词义	*a*. 讽刺的，讥笑的	She has a sarcastic tongue. 她喜欢挖苦人。

tone [təun]

核心词义	n. 音调，音质，语调	His tone is rather unfriendly. 他的口气很不友好。 This violin has very good tone. 这把小提琴的音色很好。
习惯用法	tone down 缓和，减弱	

Lesson
93

A noble gift
崇高的礼物

noble [ˈnəubl]		
核心词义	a. 高尚的，壮丽的，贵族的，高贵的	He is a noble man, we all admire him. 他是一个道德高尚的人，我们都敬佩他。
联想词汇	novel [ˈnɔvəl] n. 小说 a. 新颖的；珍奇的，异常的	

monument [ˈmɔnjumənt]		
核心词义	n. 纪念碑	A monument was erected to the memory of that great scientist. 树立了一块纪念碑纪念那位伟大的科学家。

statue [ˈstætjuː]		
核心词义	n. 塑像，雕像	The statue was cast in bronze. 这座雕像是用青铜铸的。
联想词汇	status [ˈsteitəs] n. 地位，身份，情形，状况	

liberty [ˈlibəti]		
核心词义	n. 自由	The constitution guards the liberty of people. 宪法保障人民的自由。
联想词汇	liberal [ˈlibərəl] n. 自由主义者 a. 慷慨的，不拘泥的 liberate [ˈlibəreit] v. 解放，使……获自由，释放	

present [ˈpreznt]		
核心词义	v. 赠送	We presented him a basketball on his birthday. 他生日那天我们送给他一个篮球。

sculptor [ˈskʌlptə]

核心词义	n. 雕刻家	He is one of Britain's best-known sculptors. 他是英国最有名的雕塑家之一。

actual [ˈæktjuəl]

核心词义	a. 实际的，真实的	All actual objects are concrete. 一切实际存在的物体都是具体的。
联想词汇	virtual [ˈvəːtjuəl] a. 实际上的，实质的	

copper [ˈkɔpə]

核心词义	n. 铜，铜币，铜制品	Copper conducts electricity well. 铜是电的良导体。

support [səˈpɔːt]

核心词义	v. 支撑；支援，帮助；支持，赞助	Walls support the roof. 墙支撑着屋顶。 Our school is supported by the government. 政府赞助我校的办学费用。
拓展词义	n. 支持，支撑，援助，供养	Your support has meant a lot to me during this difficult time. 在这困难时期，你的支持给了我很大的帮助。
习惯用法	in support of 帮助（支援）……，为……辩护	

framework [ˈfreimwəːk]

核心词义	n. 结构，构架，框架	The block of office buildings was built of concrete on a steel framework. 这组办公大楼是在钢结构上用混凝土建成的。
联想词汇	frame [freim] n. 框，结构，骨架 v. 给……装框子	

transport [trænsˈpɔːt]

核心词义	v. 运送，流放	A bus transported us from the airport to the city. 一辆公共汽车把我们从飞机场送到城里。

词根词缀	trans-通过 + port 港口
联想词汇	sport [spɔːt] n. 运动，游戏，运动会

site [sait]

核心词义	n. 位 置，场所，地点	The site for the new factory has not been decided yet. 新厂的地址尚未选定。
拓展词义	v. 使坐落于	It is safe to site a company here. 在这里建造工厂安全。
联想词汇	parasite ['pærəsait] n. 寄生虫，靠他人为生的人	

pedestal ['pedistl]

核心词义	n. 基 架；底座	At the very top of the steps was a bust of Shakespeare on a pedestal. 就在台阶顶端的基座上有一尊莎士比亚半身像。
联想词汇	pedestrian [pe'destriən] n. 行人；步行者	

Lesson

94

Future champions
未来的冠军

instruct [in'strʌkt]		
核心词义	v. 指导，传授	She instructed me in the use of the telephone. 她教我如何使用电话。
习惯用法	instruct sb. to do sth. 命令某人做某事	

Los Angeles [lɔs-'ændʒələs]		
核心词义	n. 洛杉矶（美国城市）	I moved from Los Angeles to San Francisco at the age of thirty. 我在30岁时从洛杉矶搬到旧金山。

reluctant [ri'lʌktənt]		
核心词义	a. 不情愿的，勉强的	He gave me a reluctant assistance. 他很不情愿地给了我帮助。

weight [weit]		
核心词义	n. 重量，体重，重担，重物	He can lift heavy weights because of his strength. 他力气大，可举起重物。 The pillars couldn't support the weight of the roof. 这些柱子无法承受屋顶的重量。
联想词汇	weigh [wei] v. 秤重量；权衡	

underwater ['ʌndə'wɔːtə]		
核心词义	a. 在水中生长的；水下的	The ship was underwater when they reached her. 他们赶到那艘船时，船已沉到水里了。

tricycle [ˈtraisikl]

核心词义	n. 三轮车	The little girl abandoned her tricycle. 那个小女孩丢弃了她的三轮车。
联想词汇	cycle [ˈsaikl] n. 循环，周期	
词根词缀	tri 三 + cycle 圈，环	

compete [kəmˈpiːt]

核心词义	v. 竞争，对抗	Some 1,000 athletes competed in 20 events. 约 1000 名运动员参加了 20 个项目的比赛。
习惯用法	compete with 与某人竞争	

yard [jɑːd]

核心词义	n. 庭院；场地，码（等于 3 英尺或 36 英寸或 0.9144 米）	You can still buy cloth by the yard in this country. 在这个国家买布还论码。 You can play outside，but you must not leave the yard. 你可以在外面玩，但不得离开院子。

gasp [gɑːsp]

核心词义	v. 喘气；渴望	The exhausted runner threw himself down and gasped. 那位筋疲力尽的赛跑运动员一头栽倒，直喘气。
拓展词义	n. 喘气	She gave a gasp of surprise. 她吃惊得大口喘气。
习惯用法	gasp for/after 喘（气）；渴望 gasp out 上气不接下气地说	
联想词汇	gas [gæs] n. 煤气，气体，毒气	

Lesson

95

A fantasy
纯属虚构

---

fantasy [ˈfæntəsi, ˈfæntəzi]

核心词义	n. 幻想故事	Everyone should indulge in fantasy on occasion. 每个人都应偶尔沉浸在想象之中。

---

ambassador [æmˈbæsədə]

核心词义	n. 大使	He is the Chinese ambassador to Japan. 他是中国驻日本大使。

---

frightful [ˈfraitful]

核心词义	a. 可怕的，令人吃惊的	These frightful experiences are branded on his memory. 这些可怕的经历深深印入他的记忆。

---

fire extinguisher [ˈfaiə-iksˈtiŋgwiʃə]

核心词义	灭火器	Kept a fire extinguisher available at all times. 任何时候都要放置即时可用的灭火器。
联想词汇	extinguish [iksˈtiŋgwiʃ] v. 使扑灭，熄灭，使不复存在 distinguish [disˈtiŋgwiʃ] v. 区别，辨别，表现突出 anguish [ˈæŋgwiʃ] n. (尤其指心理上的) 极度的痛苦	

---

drily [ˈdraili]

核心词义	ad. 枯燥无味地，冷淡	His answer looks so drily. 他的回答看起来那么冷淡。

| 联想词汇 | dry [drai] *a*. 干的，枯燥无味的，干燥的；缺水的，口渴的 *v*. 变干 |
| | daily ['deili] *a*. 每日的，日常的 *n*. 日报 |

embassy ['embəsi]

| 核心词义 | *n*. 大使馆 | He is with the French Embassy.
他在法国大使馆工作。 |

heaven ['hevən]

| 核心词义 | *n*. 天堂；上帝；极乐 | He looked at the starry heavens.
他看着布满星星的天空。
It is heaven to be here with you.
能够和你在这儿是件很愉快的事。 |

basement ['beismənt]

| 核心词义 | *n*. 地下室 | It is rather damp in his basement.
他的地下室很潮湿。 |
| 联想词汇 | base [beis] *n*. 基底 *v*. 以……作基础
basis ['beisis] *n*. 基础，根据
basic ['beisik] *n*. 基本，要素 *a*. 基本的 | |

definitely ['definitli]

| 核心词义 | *ad*. 肯定地，一定地 | The team will definitely lose if he doesn't play. 如果他不参加比赛，这个队肯定会输。 |
| 联想词汇 | finite ['fainait] *a*. 有限的，（语）限定的
defination [ˌdefi'niʃən] *n*. 定义，清晰度 | |

post [pəust]

| 核心词义 | *v*. 委派；张贴；邮寄 | We posted a guard to keep watch.
我们派了一名卫兵站岗。
Post this notice on the wall.
把这个通知贴在墙上。
He posted the letter this morning.
他今天上午把信寄出去了。 |

| 拓展词义 | *n* . 柱，邮件，岗位，职位，邮政 | There was no end to the letters pouring into the post office. 有大量的信投进了邮局。
Ask him whether he would accept the post. 问问他是否愿意就任该职。 |

shot [ʃɒt]

核心词义	*n* . 开枪，射击；子弹，炮弹；射手	He fired two shots, both missed. 他打了两枪，都没有打中。 His shot went to the right of the goal. 他一脚射门，球向球门右边飞去。
拓展词义	*a* . 颜色会变化的，用旧的	He bought a shot silk. 他买了一匹闪光的丝绸。
联想词汇	shoot [ʃuːt] *n* . 射击，发射，摄影 *v* . 射击，投射，拍摄

Lesson

96

The dead return
亡灵返乡

---

festival [ˈfestəvəl]		
核心词义	*n*. 节日，喜庆日	We spent most of the Spring Festival at home. 春节的大部分时间我们都在家过的。
联想词汇	feast [fiːst] *n*. 宴会，酒席，盛会 *v*. 大吃大喝，享用美食；款待或宴请某人	
习惯用法	Spring Festival Gala Evening 春节联欢晚会	

---

lantern [ˈlæntən]		
核心词义	*n*. 灯笼	To make a Halloween lantern, you first have to gouge out the inside of the pumpkin. 要做一个万圣节灯笼，你先得挖空这个南瓜。

---

spectacle [ˈspektəkl]		
核心词义	*n*. 壮观，场面，景象；眼镜	The spectacle greatly excited us at the time. 当时那场面令我们十分激动。
联想词汇	spectacular [spekˈtækjulə] *a*. 壮观的，惊人的